WH

- Please return items before closing time
  on the last date stamped to avoid charges.
- Renew books by phoning 01305 224311 or
  online www.dorsetforyou.com/libraries
- Items may be returned to any Dorset library.
- Please note that children's books issued on
  an adult card will incur overdue charges.

Dorset County Council
Library Service

DL/2372 dd05450

Published by Hansib Publications in 2008
London & Hertfordshire

Hansib Publications Limited
P.O. Box 226, Hertford, Hertfordshire, SG14 3WY, UK

Email: info@hansib-books.com
Website: www.hansib-books.com

A catalogue record of this book is
available from the British Library

ISBN: 978-1-906190-13-2

Printed and bound in the UK

Dedicated to
my niece Lorraine
and
my sons Jacques and Richard

Chapter one

She lay on the bed with her face buried in the pillow trying desperately to forget, to blot out the experience from her mind. That proved the difficult part; she could not forget, could never forget, it seemed to her. Worse, she hated being alone, for then the memories crowded back, haunting her, forcing her to relive the experience over again, until often she would run out, outside, anywhere, to see people going about their normal everyday tasks; to talk to someone, even. Anyone. Just to help her chase away the thoughts bedeviling her. If only she were able to rid herself of that feeling of guilt and of incompetence. Why? She asked herself. Why had she failed at the last moment? What had gone wrong? What? What? What….?

The tears blurred Helen's vision when she raised her head to look at the walls. Objects swam before her eyes then vanished in a watery haze.

At home her parents had always dismissed her as being useless, that she could do nothing right. She had tried. God knows she had tried, but always she had succeeded in making a mess of everything, as though to confirm that opinion of her. At school the teachers had said the same….Yes, she was a bright girl. If only she had set her mind to do the work, results would have been better. Oh, so much better. And there was certainly no need for all that untidiness.

What was the matter with her? How many times had she asked herself that question? She could not remember.

Sometimes she thought of running away, but could never bring herself to do it for good. Someday…..Someday she would gather sufficient courage and run away; to go somewhere far away where no one would find her. Back to the Caribbean? She did not know since she could not remember the home, nor the island which she had left with her parents when she was only seven years old to come to London.

Helen often thought of her grandmother whenever she felt so depressed. Grandmother who had been ever so kind to her, and to her brothers and sisters, and whom she had loved so much. Now grandmother was dead and there was no one to whom she could return. Even her mother had disappeared with another man, and nobody had seen her nor knew where she was now in this great metropolitan city. She might even have left England.

There was no more quarrelling since her mother left, and her father seemed a more reasonable person, sometimes, but she did not like her step-mother, Anita, who was young and rather attractive. Anita cared more about herself than about anyone else. She never seemed to hear when anyone spoke to her, and her part in any conversation almost invariably differed from the subject matter, and then one realized that she had not really been listening. She seldom paid any attention to her husband's children. And her father, once he had provided what he thought was his duty, paid little attention to his children.

Before her mother had disappeared her father would often leave the home at night for long hours and sometimes did not return till the next morning in time to change his clothes before going off to work.

All those things had played on Helen's mind, had troubled her until one day she ran away. That day, instead of going to school, the feeling had suddenly come upon her that she no longer wanted to see her parents, nor her brothers and sisters. No, not anyone whom she knew.

She had found herself walking, walking, walking, almost halfway across London. Then night had set in and she had been hungry. She had not seen the police woman until the officer had been almost upon her. She had refused to give her address, so she had been taken to the police station and had been kept there for the night.

Her father had found her, or perhaps she had told the police where she lived.. She could not remember now, but her father had come to fetch her. King's Cross, that had been how far she had walked. From Elephant and Castle to King's Cross. That had been before they had moved to Bermondsey.

Oh, God, what a place, that house in Bermondsey!

Her father had taken her home and locked her in, and she had cried and cried, so frightened had she been of being left alone. She had grown up with that same fear of being left alone. She had never wanted to live in a house again for fear of being locked in.

Her father had punished her, and that had made everything worse. He had not come in and spoken gently to her, only warning her of his intention to punish her for running away and for causing him and her mother so much anxiety. In this city where a young black person was never safe, always being picked up by the police for any imaginary offence.

No, he had simply opened the door, like a thief...yes, like a thief in the night while she was asleep and she had felt the strap across her buttocks. She had jumped up, screaming. What a terrible nightmare she had imagined that she had been having! But it had been no nightmare.

"Good for nothing!" her father had called her with each stroke of the strap. "Daughter of a whore!"

Oh, my God! Thinking of it now made her want to scream. To have said that about her mother, and to her, a young girl, a mere child. Oh, how cruel! How horribly cruel!

Was that the reason for his having treated her mother so badly? So offensively?

Yes, her mother did go out often, but that was because her father never took her anywhere. And he did not himself remain at home either. There were nights when she and her brothers and sister were alone in the house for almost half the night. That was not fair because it threw a heavy burden of responsibility upon her. If she were frightened she dared not let the younger ones see it.

She remembered certain incidents; the way her father used to beat her mother. Holding her by the shoulders and knocking her head against the wall. Kick her till she would crawl at his feet begging for mercy. Begging him not to treat her that way in the presence of the children. But he would stop only in his own good time, when he had felt satisfied, or exhausted.

She remembered, also, the first time that her mother had ran away. She had taken the children with her, the two boys, her sister and herself. They had had to live in a large room close to Victoria Park, in Bow, the East End of London and the children had had to sleep on the floor. That had not been so bad because it had been a good summer. She remembered, for on Wednesday and Saturday afternoons she used to hear the noise from the young people and the bands which played for the open air dances in the Park. Some nights her mother would put them on the bed to sleep and she would herself sleep on the floor.

Those were the nights when Fred, the long distance truck driver from Liverpool, slept in the room. After a while Fred and her mother, imagining that they were asleep, would start to whisper in the dark, and then the terrible heavy breathings and sucking noises would come from the corner where they were, and she would hear her mother groaning as though labouring under a heavy burden, and she would hear Fred calling her mother those horrible names.

God, why are people so beastly to one another?

Those nights would be fraught with danger for her and her mind would be vivid with fearful imaginings.

One evening Fred had come in drunk while her mother had been out, and he had held her close. pawing her, breathing heavily down the back of her neck. Then Fred had unbuttoned the front of his trousers and had taken out that thing! He had tried to lift up her dress and she had screamed. Fred had taken fright and had tried to soothe her, telling her that it had only been a game; that he would stop if she did not want to play the game with him. But she had not stopped screaming until he had released her. She had been thirteen years then, but a big girl for her age, so she had often been told, with her bust already full and womanly.

Her father had discovered where they lived and he had beaten her mother and had taken them back to the house. He had beaten her again when they had got home; so badly that some white neighbours, who had heard screams had called the police, imagining that he had intended to kill her.

Her father had been sent to prison for that offence and they had all been so terribly ashamed.

Her mother had ran away the day her father came out of prison, and had left them with the neighbour next door. She must have been terribly afraid to have done a thing like that, deserting them. But her father had found out that she had gone away with the man whom she had been seeing all along.

Her father had married again, Anita, a woman much younger than himself, after his divorce. When the boys had come of age she persuaded her father to get them to join the armed forces. One was in the army and the other in the air force.

All those things she had related to Roy, her husband, one night after she had asked him about himself and about his home in St. Vincent, and had heard him tell of his affection for his parents. She had felt a twinge of envy and had tried to conceal it, but it had come out nonetheless.

"Our childhood has been so different" she had confessed dejectedly "So very different." Then she had cried out with a vehemence that had caused Roy to turn to her in alarm "I hate my father! I hate him! He used to treat us so abominably! I saw him kick my mother once, right across the room! I don't care how she might have done to him, he had no right to do that in our presence. He never saw that she had to look for someone because of the way he used to behave. Some men think that they can do whatever they want to their women, or their wives and they must simply sit back and accept it. Well, it was not so with my mother, and my father realized that when he had kicked her that night."

"Good gracious! Was he drunk?"

"Drunk? If he had been that would have been some excuse. No, he was as sober as a saint". She paused a moment, then added "You know, one night he came into the room and found my mother preparing to light the fire. It was a cold night in the middle of winter, mind you. He walked up to her and put out the fire. 'If you want warmth' he said, 'go out in the garden and dig! That'll warm you.' The old bastard!"

Roy placed his arm about her shoulders to console her. "Helen, you must not say that about your father. After all, he is still your father".

"Father? Father? That old bastard! Come to think of it, although I sympathize with my mother she was no different. And that step-mother of ours, that's another one. Always telling us that we were in the way; wanting us to clear out. Either join the army or air force or get married. Oh, God! What a choice! What a childhood, eh?"

She shook her head miserably and presently began to sob, silently, her bosom heaving as though all the sorrow, confined in the depths of her body, had been too heavy to bring to the surface.

Roy's arm was still about her shoulders. "Poor Helen....Poor Helen....You've had a terrible time and you're upset. Please don't worry about it; it's all over now."

She felt happy being with him, she told him. He had treated her kindly, like a human being, for the first time in her life someone cared about her. She wished there was some way to repay his kindness and attention. He protested, exhorting her not to talk like that. After all, she was his wife, and he was there to do whatever needed to be done.

"I know all that, Roy." Then with a wave of the hand which encompassed the entire room, she continued "You've given me a home where I am welcome. Everything that I have now, you gave me. I sometimes wonder if I deserve all this, or why. Do you know something? Until I met you I never knew what wearing good clothes was like. No, listen to me; it is true, Roy. What I mean is, until I met you I had never met anyone before who cared what I wore, or what I looked like. All the black men, and whites, too, I had known before could hardly wait for the moment when they would jump into bed with me. So what was the use of clothes? They only wanted me to get out of them as fast as possible. And you want to know something else? Not one would give anything, but they always wanted, always expected, always demanded something."

She paused now, thinking how wrong it was to have caused him such pain. To talk of the other men whom she had known was not right. She told herself that, in fairness to him, she ought to have spared him that, she said now, in a tone intended to mollify, to ease the hurt and pain, as if that were possible. She realized with a pained awareness her indiscretion. "At least, Roy, my darling, you were decent enough to marry me. How many men would have done the same in the circumstances, eh? How many? None of those I knew before. The...."

She stopped abruptly, aware that she had already said too much. She looked at him intently, her eyes beseeching the forgiveness which she felt she would understand were he not to give it.

He said nothing, only looked away to hide the hurt which would show. She would not, could not blame him. After all, what man, with however refined an upbringing such as Roy, however broadminded, she told herself, likes to learn afterwards that the woman whom he has married, has known other men?

The first revelation of that fact sent a pain shooting through every fibre of Roy's body, and he shuddered as with a sudden revulsion. And Helen observed now, of a sudden, that he had receded into his strangely remote silence, a silence so deep and so remote that she, that no one could reach him. It was always like that with him, she remembered now, whenever he was hurt.

She became overwhelmed with sorrow and remorse. "I love you, Roy", she said presently with a warmth of feeling that, even at so remote a distance, spiritually, from her, did not escape his notice. He looked up to behold her smiling that soothing captivating smile that had so often charmed him. "Yes, you've been good to me", she continued, and caressed the arm that he had removed from around her shoulders. "I only wish that some day I'll be able to make up for all you've done for me. This country is hell, Roy. Maybe when we return to your island, yes. I hope to God I don't spoil it for you".

Chapter two

Yet she had spoilt it, she told herself now. She had wanted the child and she could not help feeling guilty about having lost it. After all those months! And she had disappointed him in the end. Badly! Was she ever going to do anything right? Was she ever going to do anything worthwhile? Useless! Useless! And it's true, too. Yes, it is! He had wanted it so much and you had to let him down. You carried it inside you for nine months….nine whole months….and at the last moment you had to go and lose it. You fool! Won't anything good come of you? You are hopeless! Absolutely hopeless! A simple thing like that and you had to go and spoil it.

She would have been a pretty girl, too. Roy had often said that he wanted a girl, for there were not many girls in his family.

Oh, you are useless, Helen! Indeed, you are. Can't do anything right. Good-for-nothing. Nothing you ever do is right.

She wished she were able to fall asleep and never wake up again. She had disappointed him, oh, ever so badly. She felt she would always let him down.

The little girl, her daughter, would have been four months old to-day.

She did not hear him come in. He had not found her in the sitting room and, fancying that she was asleep, he had opened the door to the bedroom silently, only to discover her lying with her back to him, facing the wall. He went up to her softly, on tiptoe.

"Oh, Helen, you've been crying again?" His voice carried concern and alarm "What is the matter, sweetheart?"

"I was lonely" she said, without turning to face him. "I don't like being by myself." It was almost like a plea and he put his hand out instinctively to touch her arm, to caress it, really. "I don't like being on my own."

"But, sweetheart, I have to be at college. You know that."

"Yes, I know, Roy." She was asking for forgiveness, for some kind of understanding of her plight. She said now "Oh, I am horrible, aren't I? I'm horrible and selfish, I know."

"No, Helen. You're not. And I didn't say that."

"No, but you implied it."

He shook his head and caressed her arm some more. She was like that sometimes, he remembered; an act, a word of contrition, then she would return to the attack. To-day he did not feel inclined to be in any mood for argument. He felt pity for her, sorry that she had to be alone some of the time.

He said "Helen, look sweetheart..." Then he saw the baby's clothes on the bed beside her. She Had been lying down on them, and he saw them as she made a movement with her hands. He stumbled, at a loss what to say. Then "Helen...? I...shall put them away." The words came haltingly as he stretched out his hand to gather up the tiny garments.

Her scream shattered the quiet and he stepped back instinctively. "No! No! Leave me alone! Leave me alone, please!"

He moved farther away, puzzled and confused, wondering what to do next. He said now "I'll.....I'm going to make some coffee. Shall I bring you a cup?"

He was sure that was not quite what he wanted to say, and he regretted it. He regretted having to reveal the confusion in his mind. Oh, God!

She turned over on her back and stared intently at him, as though trying to make out whom it really could be standing there; that person looking at her. Then the eyes lost him, held nothing. It was as though nothing was there at all. Again that feeling of inward helplessness, of utter puzzlement crept over him, gripped him for a moment as though wanting to paralyze him. He shook himself free of that fear which threatened even now to engulf him. He saw her eyes move, and he realized that she had not bothered to answer his question.

He repeated the question and once again felt the stupidity of it, the helplessness seeming to overpower him. He observed the shadow of a smile hovering briefly at the corners of her mouth, and she nodded, slowly, almost imperceptibly. He felt a little encouraged, and announced, more cheerful now "I'll tell you what I'll do. I'll make a little snack before we cook. How's that, eh?"

He said "we" although he knew very well that she was never interested in cooking. That had been one of his disappointments, that not only could she not cook, but disliked cooking intensely. She would try it on occasion, but that only rarely.

She nodded once again, and there was that smile again, playing on her lips. It occurred to her that he still, sometimes, chose to regard her as a child; treat her as such, even. But, she told herself, she must not complain; had no right to complain, really, for, after all, had she not given him cause to treat her so? She recalled the first time he had asked her to make some coffee. Nescafe, simple to make, yet she had succeeded in making a horrible mess of it. She had watched him painfully force himself to drink it. Now he no longer asked her to do any such things. He did the cooking himself each evening after he returned from college, and tried to hide his disappointment.

"I am useless, aren't I?" she had said to him when he had first discovered that she knew not her way about the kitchen. "I wish you had married someone else; someone more capable. I honestly do."

He had been unable to conceal his annoyance then, and had blurted out "Oh, for Christ sake! We're not all gifted, you know," knowing not how to combat her excessive self criticism, yet knowing that, on numerous occasions and in moments of utter despair, he wished that it had been as she had said.

"I don't even try" she persisted and that irritated him.

Exasperated now he cried out "Well, I'm not stopping you, am I?"

"Oh, you know very well that I'll make a mess of it. Like I do everything else."

He had tried. God knows he had tried, repeatedly and in diverse ways, to find some means whereby he could make her get rid of that feeling of incompetence and of inferiority, that preoccupation with self-chastisement, but. no, he had almost given up for, unconsciously or otherwise, she persisted in setting up a barrier against all attempts to assist her; so that he now tried less, for it had occurred to him that the effort and the strain upon himself was hampering his own work, and that if something, some miracle were not to happen soon to reverse that trend, then he would most certainly go insane.

Outside snow flakes danced crazily past the window.

Sitting at the table now, eating, she said, looking quizzically at him, "Roy, I think I ought to go out to work soon. Don't you think so? Perhaps it would help. I'm strong enough now. And I won't feel so lonely then."

"If you really feel up to it."

"Yes, I think so."

Now, as he gave the matter some further thought, he repeated aloud "Perhaps it won't be such a bad idea after all. But, what would like to do?"

"I don't know, Roy. Anything I can get, I suppose. Jobs are difficult to find nowadays."

"Still, not just anything, surely. You must have some idea what you want to do. What did you do before?"

It had come to him, then, that he had never before enquired of her employment. Almost as though it had not really mattered at all, so much taken up had he been with her from the very beginning. Or had it been that, really? He did not know why. It had simply never occurred to him. And then, everything had happened so suddenly.

She answered now, almost apologetically, "Oh, a silly job, really. Filing clerk." And she chuckled as though to conceal her embarrassment.

He was surprised. "Where the devil was that?"

"Oh, some firm in the City."

He laughed softly. "Well, you wouldn't want to do any such thing again. It all sounds so boring to me."

"Oh, Christ, no!" She laughed now for the first time in many weeks. He looked at her and smiled. "What a place that was!" she added

They had been a strange crowd at that place, she recalled. Never had been able to have a decent conversation with anyone there. The firm exported commodities to a number of countries throughout the world, but principally to Germany and France. Three Directors and not one had ever crossed the Channel either on business or on holiday. She had started to learn French once for letters to and from the firm had always to be sent for translation. She could hardly contain her surprise when they had discovered her ambition.

"What you want to learn that for?" one of the Directors had asked.

"Oh, they were a right lot, they were" Helen said. "I suppose it must have seemed strange to them, me, a black girl with ambition.

Roy laughed. He could well imagine the people there. Three years in England had revealed more than enough for him to harbour any illusions of the "image" of that great race of men, the descendants of Shakespeare, and of Milton and Hawkins and Drake, Nelson, and the others. What could have changed a people so? Spineless and without much spirit now. Ah, well....He chuckled, looking over at Helen. She would have made an excellent actress, he thought, listening to her mimicking her former employers and the staff there.

"Well, what would you like to do?" he asked again.

She shrugged her shoulders. "Oh, I'll find something. I suppose I'll go out on Monday and start looking around."

Roy, also, laughed and shrugged his shoulders. "Okay. I'll leave it to you."

"Yes," she said, and rose from the table to contemplate the snowflakes now drifting heavily downwards, "it will do me good. I'm sure it will."

Chapter three

The snow continued to fall and it was one of the severest winters that Roy had experienced since his arrival; the worse, too, so the radio, television and newspapers informed everyone, for a very long time. And then there were the industrial disruptions. to crown it all. The media, never at a loss for slogans, called it 'The Winter of Discontent.' It was certainly not original, being a quotation from Shakespeare, but Roy could not remember which of the plays. Great chap, Shakespeare, Roy thought. Don't know what the English would have done without him. They have not produced anyone worthwhile since, not in playwrights, anyway. Maybe that's why they're so miserable. He chuckled to himself.

Helen caught a cold, but Doctor Franklin, from Grenada, a cousin of Roy's, treated her and she was well again within a week. She expressed her gratitude for having been given such personal attention. She had always imagined that only the very wealthy and the socially privileged had their doctors call daily upon them. Here she was, enjoying greater fortune, for the doctor was a member of the family.

Doctor Franklin told Roy about the winter of nineteen forty-seven, when everything had been frozen and there had been a scarcity of fuel, even, to enable one to keep comfortably warm. Many people had died that winter, as though another plague had visited the country. It had all seemed so terribly unfair, such a burden coming so soon after the war and when so few houses were available. Most of them had been badly damaged by the bombs and sadly in need of repair. Worse, everything imaginable had been in short supply in the shops, and on ration, too. Misery and deprivation had been the commodities in plentiful supply, and free.

"You have no idea how we suffered," said Doctor Franklin's wife, who was English.

Doctor Franklin said "It seems all the people of this country do, is suffer."

They were sitting near the fire, drinking coffee and chocolate. When Doctor Franklin and his wife left, Helen got up from the chair and fetched a rug and sat down on the floor staring into the fire. It came to her that she ought to tell Roy about the people where she now worked, for she had found a job after much searching. He appeared so deep in thought that she wondered whether she ought to disturb him. She decided against it. Not just now, she thought; she would wait for the appropriate time.

She must remember to tell him about Dickson, the man in charge of the dry goods warehouse; the seedy little man with the spectacles always on the tip of his nose, constantly coughing, perpetually complaining, yet forever falling over himself to do the 'Governor's' bidding. The more he bent over backwards to please, the more the 'Governor' found fault with his work, incessantly shouting at old Dickson. And Dickson—he was in his sixtieth year—not knowing what to do and at a loss what to say.

Dickson would look at Helen with supplication in his eyes, and moan and bewail his misfortunes. In that manner Helen had discovered that Dickson had been with the company for forty years, yet he was still being treated as though he was a juvenile. He had given all his working life to the company, and what had been his reward? To be bullied about and to be blamed for everything that went wrong, whether or not he had had anything to do with whatever had happened. He was expected to carry out the duties of Company Director, stock keeper, warehouseman, foreman, motor mechanic, messenger. Tea-boy, detective, and a host of other unmentionable things as well.

Helen sympathized with him, for at his age there seemed nothing that old Dickson could do about his predicament. He had a wife, and his two daughters had married and left, one for Canada and the other to South Africa, but they had never written to him of late years. He did not know whether they were still alive. All that disturbing news on television and in the newspapers made him think often of Janet, the one who had migrated to South Africa. He did not even have an address to write to, if he had had a mind to write, which he did not, seeing as how they had treated him.

Dickson confessed to Helen that he had not yet completed the payments for the mortgage on his house. The Company had lent him part of the money and he was soon due for retirement. Oh, he will have finished the payments by then, but it was something of a burden still on his mind. No, fate had not treated him kindly. He had not much money saved and he faced the remainder of his life in retirement with an awful dread.

Helen often wondered during those moments when he unfolded his heart to her, why Dickson had remained and had not sought alternative employment while he had still been a young man. Like the young West Indian from Grenada, Phil, who had come three months ago to work in the warehouse, packing furniture and china for shipment overseas.

In the second week with the Company Phil had found himself being given some menial tasks to perform - washing the 'Governor's' car, running small errands, taking the 'Governor's' suits, shirts and shirt collars to the cleaners. Phil did not say anything for the first two weeks. The third week the 'Governor' brought Phil pillow cases and bed sheets to take to the laundry across the road and Phil had stared at the dirty pile in disbelief, observing the sperm and menstruation-soiled sheets, and he had turned his back and had walked out in disgust.

"That's a job for your wife, man", was all he had said, not angrily, for he felt himself beyond anger; not even raising his voice beyond his conversational tone of everyday speech, smiling as though he had at last encountered a joker par excellence. Only his eyes had held that unassailable black pride and superiority.

He had taken up his hat and had said simply, familiarly, almost, "Cherio, folks. It was nice knowing you all." And had walked out and away, not even asking for his wages, nor for his employment card. Just walked away and had never returned.

No, she would not tell Roy about that. To drive all the way from Roehampton to Blackfriars with a parcel of soiled linen simply to save a few pence, because then he could send the things to be cleaned along with the towels and overalls from the office and the warehouse so that the Company would pay the bill. How mean could a man get! No, she would not soil Roy's ears with such gross indecencies.

Old Dickson's remarks had made her very angry. "I don't know" he had said. "They come to this country and we give them work, and they expect to be treated like kings."

She had smiled bitterly. Old Dickson, scraping the floor with his bows, bowing and accepting every humiliation till there seemed not a fragment of his humanity left; his manhood, his dignity reduced lower than that of the vilest worm. A "Yes, guv" man, as she had often heard Roy's friend, Elton, remark. How disgustingly lower was Old Dickson prepared to reduce himself further!

She shook her head. She certainly will not remain at that place for long, that's for sure. Just long enough to get used to working again, to rebuild her confidence, then she would find something else to do much more to her liking. Much more....What was the word? Conducive, that's it, to her nature.

A strong healthy youngman like Phil, and Dickson had called the washing of cars and the taking of soiled linen to the laundry, "work!" My God! She told herself that if ever she were to gain any position of authority in this land, she would show them. The Dicksons as well. Perhaps it was just as well the people of this land were seeing to it that the West Indians did not get on very far, did not get that break that would give them some power and authority in this country. They must have realized a long time ago the kind of people the West Indians are. But that cannot last for long. Those who were born in this country would certainly demand more, demand what is their due. What then? They will have to be accommodated, that's for sure.

And thinking of it now she hated the Dicksons of this land. The country was swarming with them. "Yes, guv." "No, guv." Christ, how she detested them! Where was their dignity? Their self respect? Won't the working classes ever learn? She would show them one day. Yes, she would, indeed.

Was it that they were such a disciplined people? She was convinced now that that was not the case. Rather, they were obedient, like trained animals; they responded to authority, to the person in authority, regardless of the complexion of the person who wielded that authority. They were truly "Yes, guv" people.

Those thoughts strengthened her. She looked over at Roy and of a sudden felt the confidence that she had so desperately needed come seeping into her and gradually begin to course through her veins. She saw him smile, but seemed uncertain whether or not the smile was meant for her, for he was still gazing into the depths of the fire.

"What is it?" she ventured to ask.

He chuckled, seemingly pleased with the thoughts with which he was occupied. "I was thinking of the paper that I wrote on Swift," he said. "Mr. Jameson liked it tremendously. He thought it was the best thing that I had done so far."

Helen said "He seems very fond of you. From what you have been telling me. He's always giving you encouragement."

He rose to fetch his briefcase and took out some sheets of paper. "Here," he said. "Take a look at it."

Helen looked at the written work. "But....it's a play," she said. "I thought you told me it was an essay."

Roy laughed. "As a matter of fact, Mr. Jameson warned me against attempting any such thing in the examination room. I told him that it was only an experiment, really. Of course I couldn't possibly do that in the examination room."

Helen noted the title: 'Swift Murders To Dissect' and then proceeded to read. Swift was on trial for his life. Dr. Johnson was the Presiding Judge, Pope the Defence Counsel, and Colly Cibber, the Prosecuting Attorney. The case against Swift was powerfully presented. He was accused of misanthropy, of dissecting human beings solely for the purpose of his own experiment, and of labeling the various pieces and giving them names such as Pride, Folly, Envy, Jealousy and a host of other designations until there appeared nothing that was of any good in human nature. The sexual act he had found to be obnoxious.

Pope pleaded brilliantly on behalf of his friend. He referred to the 'Journal To Stella' and to 'The Battle of the Books' to demonstrate that Swift was not, could never be, in fact, what the Prosecutor claimed him to be. But he pleaded to no avail. The jury found Swift guilty, but made a strong recommendation for mercy for, they claimed, Swift was not in his right state of mind. The newssheets circulating the Coffee Houses proclaimed in their banner headlines 'Swift Guilty, But Insane.'

Helen agreed that the work had been very cleverly executed. She liked it, she said, but confessed that she had never seen Swift in that particular light; had never arrived at those conclusions from her reading of the books. Roy seemed anxious to have her opinion on his value as a potential critic and she shrugged vaguely.

"It's difficult to say, to pass judgment' she told him. "We see things in a different light."

She recalled her own unique interpretation of English Literature when she had been studying for her Advance Level G.C.E. She, coming from a Caribbean colonial background could not possibly see the same things as the English student, even though she had grown up in England. Only when she had recognized that had she been able to come to terms with how she had to proceed with her work; that she was not incorrect, but merely differed from her tutor's and her classmates' interpretation.

"That's how it ought to be" Roy said. "No two people can be expected to come to the same conclusion. Experiences differ. One's idea on life, too, conditions one's way of viewing and seeing things."

"Who am I, then, to say that the other's point of view is wrong?"

He shrugged. "It does not greatly matter, Helen. One can only regard another's work as a contribution to that understanding. The more points of view, the greater the value of that contribution."

Helen smiled. "With that I agree."

"Then....?"

"Yours is a very interesting point of view. Original, really. I like it."

He laughed." Mr. Jameson thinks I should send it somewhere. He says the BBC might like it. What do you think?"

She appeared somewhat perplexed. "I don't know…I mean…Well…" she shrugged her shoulders. "You never can tell. They put out enough that's uninteresting. This might be a breath of fresh air, for a change. Who knows?"

"I wonder how much they would pay?"

Helen admitted to having no idea. "Just send it to them", she suggested after a moment of reflection. "You have nothing to lose."

"Yes, I'll do that. Ass you say, I have nothing to lose." He brightened at the thought of perhaps having his play accepted. "It would be fun if they accepted it." He paused then looked at her. "Of course, you'll have to type it for me. I can't send it away like that. My writing is none too easy to read as it is. Can you do that at your office for me?"

'I can't type," she told him.

"What?"

"You heard me." She tried to hide her embarrassment behind a smile. "I said I cannot type."

"You're not serious, Helen."

"I am, you know. " She laughed nervously now, apologetic.

"But…I don't understand. What do you do at work, then?

"Me?" She laughed again, a little frightened at what she had dreaded telling him all along. She gathered sufficient courage to say "I do the filing. Mess around generally, and make the tea, sometimes."

"What are you talking about, Helen? Messing about? Make the tea?" He almost shouted the words at her. "What the hell am I hearing, girl?"

"Well, yes." She wished to appear calm and to sound matter-of-fact for she saw that Roy was indeed put out. Shaken, really. "That's what I do in truth. It's only a temporary job, until I get something better to do."

"Don't talk stupidness, woman!" He was on his feet almost at once, pacing the room and muttering to himself. "But, what the hell is this at all? Eh, eh! What am I hearing now?"

She laughed softly to herself, wanting to retain some control over the situation with which she was now confronted, Roy's disappointment with her. "What's the matter, Roy? It's not so bad as it sounds. Why don't you sit down, man? You're making me nervous."

"Oh, shut up, woman! And let me think this out."

"Don't you shout at me! Who do you think you are, anyway?"

"Who? You ask who?" He walked deliberately over to her and stared down at her where she sat, so calm that the anger got the better of him.

"You want to know who I am, do you?"

"Don't come near me...." She cowered away from him and raised her hands as though to ward off a blow. "I'm warning you. I'll scream if you hit me."

"Hit you? Why should I hit you, woman?" He continued to stare at her, but he had mastered his anger now, and he stepped back, shaking his head at the folly of it all. "Woman", he said now with a chuckle, "you are not.....Anyway, what are we quarrelling for?"

She darted a dubious look at him, then smiled, but hesitantly. "You frightened me for a moment. I thought you were going to hit me, Roy, I honestly did."

"What for? Why should I do a thing like that? To you? "

She did not know, she said. "You might, just almost might have done it."

He said "I'm sorry, then, if I frightened you."

"That's alright, then." She said, still dubious about him and wanting to be certain that he was not really angry with her. "I honestly cannot type, Roy." She deemed herself bold enough now to drive home the reality of her incapacities. "I told you before that I was completely useless, but you didn't want to believe me. Now you know."

He shook his head as he looked at her with sadness in his eyes, it appeared to her, for he was aware now that she spoke the truth. Clearly she needed help, however much she pretended to the contrary.

"No one is completely useless in this world, Helen. We simply have to develop our capabilities, that's all." For a moment he appeared to retreat into thoughtfulness, then presently he asked her "What did you do at school, then? And at home? Oh, I know that you came to this country very young. Oh, Christ! "He had heard of the problems of the West Indian children in the British schools, how they had tried to destroy them. "Haven't you any G.C.Es? Yes, of course you have. What I mean is, didn't you learn any skills at school?"

"Apart from the G. C. Es, no. I only have four of those, and two at Advanced Level, biology and maths. I wanted to study some more, but I had leave school to look after the younger children."

"Jesus Christ!" He struck his fist against the palm of his hand and began to pace the floor again. A moment later he stopped abruptly. "This England, you see...Huh! We are living in the twentieth century, in a so-called advanced society, a Welfare State, Helen...."

She turned away her head impatiently, Hadn't she been made aware of that paradox often enough? After all, she had grown up in this country. But not to allow that painful knowledge to cloud her other achievements, she told him "I got distinctions in Maths. It has always been my best subject. Literature was second."

His attention wandered and she saw that look in his eyes which always indicated that he was deep in thought. A moment later he shook his head as though to dismiss some thought that sought to plague him.

"Well," he said at last, "you'll have to return to school. We can't have that kind of thing in my family. They'd laugh at me at home."

"I'm not exactly dumb, you know."

"I didn't say that."

"Well, I just thought I'd remind you. You have no idea how boring it was being by myself here, all day long, waiting for you to come home. I just wanted something to do, that's all. Does it really matter what I do?"

"Yes, to me it does. Making tea! Filing clerk!"

"I don't want to go back to school, Roy."

"Well, you'll have to go. Much better to learn something worthwhile than making tea and doing the filing"

"I don't have to do anything, you know. And you cannot force me."

He paid no attention to her. He said "Well, we'll see about that. To-morrow I shall investigate which school will be best for you. I must place you somewhere."

"I won't go!"

"You'll do as I say."

"I won't!"

"Alright, we'll see about that."

"What would I be returning to do, anyway?"

He had in mind Accountancy, he told her, since she was good at Maths.

"Roy, are you serious?" He assured that he had never intended it to be a joke. "It would mean having to give up my job."

"You call that a job? Making tea and doing the filing?"

"Anyway, I can't start before September."

"That's when I intend you to start."

"I didn't say I would go, you know, she thought to remind him. There was already a mellowing in her tone of voice and it occurred to Roy that that last remark was intended merely as a request for confirmation that he was, indeed, serious.

He smiled. "No, but you will."

"We'll both be at college, then. I won't be able to do any house work and to go to school as well."

"We'll manage when the time comes," he said, and smiled for he saw that she was already coming to his way of thinking.

She turned again to contemplate the fire and wondered whether she was wrong to reveal how useless she was. She was unhappy with the knowledge that, now that he had discovered her faults that it would in some unaccountable way affect their relationship. She saw it as a distinct possibility and was surprised that, though she was displeased about it, she nevertheless harboured no fears for whatever might happen. In some vague way which she would never be able to define she knew she would be prepared for it; that she would not even resist it however seriously their relationship might be affected. In seeking the meaning for that feeling her mind went over some of her encounters with Roy's friends. Always, in their company, she had been made aware, listening to their conversation and to their discussions, how painfully inadequate had been the care lavished upon her by her parents. She did not even consider her step-mother. Either deliberately or unconsciously her parents had often forced that knowledge upon her until, on occasions, she would feel not only left out, but altogether ignored, so that her first impulse was to run out of the house. But she could not very well do that, even though she wanted to. Instead she always found an excuse for leaving the room.

In such moments she harshly blamed her parents for their neglect. All she had ever heard at home were political sermons from her father and his friends. She could not feel the way that her father did so passionately about the islands—the break-up of the Federation, the inter-island rivalries, the personalities whom her father liked or disliked. All those things were too remote for her. For her father nothing else mattered.

Listening to Roy and his friends had made her aware as well that one had to be equipped to be able to participate fully and responsibly, otherwise one would soon discover that, in any society, any form of government that one had decided upon, one would find oneself doing the most menial, the most pedestrian of tasks. For then one would have been insufficiently suited for anything else, for nothing more constructive. Leaders and citizens, she had often heard Roy hold forth, had to be thoroughly educated in order that the leaders might lead and the government govern effectively. For how else would the ordinary citizen understand and appreciate what their leaders were attempting to do, or asking them to do? An uneducated public would be an ignorant public in every sense of the word, and would feel cut off, would feel that they did not belong. And that was not only bad, but decidedly dangerous. Unproductive, even.

She pondered those things now and without turning her head she said, quietly and casually, "I wish I had had your upbringing, Roy."

"We cannot all be fortunate, Helen," he said and placed a hand upon her shoulder.

He believed that once a person had discovered that something important had been missing from his life that person's duty was to set about putting things right as best as possible. There were people, he told Helen, who attended lectures, and who were old enough to be his parents. For such people he had the highest regard. That kind of decision, to pursue an academic career so late in life required a tremendous amount of discipline.

"I understand all that, Roy," she told him by way of explanation. "Some people might be just lucky enough to be able to do it, even at that advanced age. But for most of us, we are too busy trying to make ends meet even to find the time to look after ourselves properly, let alone to further our education."

"Well, at least you have one thing in your favour, you are still young."

Helen shook her head at the thought of the irony that was her life, and she chuckled. "I wish my parents had talked to me like that. I really wish they had. What I have achieved at school was of my own efforts. Sometimes I think that they are happier when we are not trying, the teachers, I mean; when we are not ambitious. They have an easier time, then. They really prefer it when the children at school are troublesome and disruptive. They get more money—danger money, I suppose. It is rare, Roy, very rare to get a white teacher who is committed to his profession; it's just a job to them, and the less trouble they take about it, the better for them. That's how I see it. And if you are black, you're not supposed to want anything worthwhile from life. Nothing academic, nothing too ambitious. They actually discourage you. You have to go through that system, Roy, to appreciate how they set their hearts on destroying a black pupil. It's crazy! Parents in the West Indies should let their children get their early education out there first, before bringing them to this country."

He had heard much about that, and had even read Bernard Coad's booklet, which had recently been published. The English were making a fuss about Coad, treating him as if he were God's gift to the universe, lionizing him so. He told Helen about him. He had attended one of Coad's speaking engagements at the University.

"Is he still in England?"

"Last I heard he had returned home."

"Well, at least he knew what was best for him."

"Well, we are all hoping so."

Helen said now "Oh, I wish I had had someone to guide me. I am sure I would have accomplished more. I never told you, Roy, but what I did accomplish was because I had to compete with some of the boys and girls in my class. I had to show them."

He said, reassuringly, hopefully, "The future is too full of possibilities, Helen, to allow yourself to dwell on the past. Don't get stuck there. Together we will achieve all that we set out to do."

Again she smiled. Not for the first time had she observed his encouragement, his optimism. "Not even our politicians seem to think like you, Roy," she confessed with a touch of regret. "It's too depressing even to listen to them."

He laughed, for he, too, had been made aware of that. "One thing I have discovered, Helen, is that Europeans are unqualified pessimists. Almost as though they cannot help it. They are like people who have exhausted all their possibilities and know not what to do."

"They cannot" Helen said. "They're prisoners of their own history, their own ideological propaganda."

Chapter four

The wintry weather dragged on into the early months of Spring, and then abruptly came to an end. That Summer Helen and Roy went to Dublin. Roy fell in love with the city where everyone went about life as casually as the Caribbean islanders are accustomed to do, as talkative, as argumentative and as talented. It was Helen's first journey away from England since she arrived from the Caribbean and she clung to Roy as though she were frightened that someone, or something might abduct her, or do something much worse she knew not what. The experience left her reflective for a time and subdued throughout the Summer.

Roy wondered what had happened to her. She did not talk about what occupied her mind and he felt no inclination to intrude. He was conscious of the fact that something, some conflict, perhaps, kept her mentally and spiritually occupied, and he deemed it prudent to allow her to resolve whatever was her dilemma. She was wont to get easily irritated of late and when the Autumn approached and the time for her enrolment drew near, she grew increasingly morose. He imagined that she still resented having to return to college. That was too bad; she would have to get used to the idea.

He had received a number of invitations to speak at several places and those would occupy him for a while and would offer some diversions to Helen as well. The first engagement, as he called it, was to the members of an organization which concerned itself with cultural matters. It was a subject dear to Roy's heart and afterwards he asked Helen what she thought about it.

She smiled, it seemed to him, distantly. "It was good" she said.

They were walking towards the underground station, and he turned to look at her. She struck him as being a trifle remote. Perhaps she was musing, churning over in her mind some of the things that he had said. He hoped he had not sounded unduly sentimental, a little too poetic, perhaps? He remained shrouded in his own thoughts for a while, then, a moment later, he spoke his thoughts aloud.

"Strange, isn't it," he said with a wry chuckle. "I come here to study and I find myself playing two roles, student and teacher."

"I wish you wouldn't keep saying that!" Helen blurted out, so vehemently that he turned to look at her in astonishment. "It's not my fault, is it?"

The outburst had had him to stop abruptly, surprise and hurt showing in his countenance. "What's the matter, Helen? What have I said or done wrong this time?"

"You will keep rubbing it in, won't you?"

He shook his head in disbelief. Of late, he recalled, he had to be increasingly mindful of what he said, for the least unguarded remark or observation, however innocently meant, was taken as a personal affront.

"Look, Helen, "he said now but with a gesture which described the futility of any explanation, for he had been made aware of her cynicism as she turned her head away in disdain. "I was simply thinking of these people who are supposed to know it all, you know. The nearest thing on the market these days, the "Experts." Nothing happens these days but that some "Expert" is brought in to explain, to give his opinion on the subject. After more than three hundred years of ruling it over us, of governing those one-time colonies, they have suddenly realized that they know nothing about us. They know nothing because they considered us to be nothing, unimportant. They could not be bothered to try to understand anything about us. After all, when you come to consider it, why should they? They were the ones who were supposed to have everything to offer, not us. It's really crazy, you know. People can go into another's country and never for one moment imagine that they can learn anything from the people whom they have conquered."

He laughed, in an effort to put Helen at her ease, but she showed no inclination to be ameliorated, keeping her head turned away from him as though he had never spoken.

Some moments later, she turned to face him. "You seem to take delight in making me feel awful, don't you?" she observed with a harshness of tone that he found to be unreasonable, and which caused him some vexation. "You did not have to marry me, you know."

"Come on, Helen, be serious. I was not referring to you. You know that very well. So how did you come into the picture, anyway?"

She pretended not to hear. She had that knack which enabled her to hold on to a belief, a point of view in any discussion with which she was opposed, to hold on to the last word of her sentence and to return to it no matter how irrelevant or how sadly mistaken she was about what was said.

"It was not your problem," she said now. "I would have managed somehow. You didn't have to marry me if you considered me not educated enough by your standards."

"Oh, for Christ sake, Helen!" he cried out in irritation, waving his hand and unaware that his voice had carried, for a couple turned to look back at them, then whispered among themselves.

That irritated Roy the more and his irritation turned to annoyance with Helen for having caused him to depart from his accustomed composure. Neither of them spoke for the remainder of the journey home. It were as though both from that moment had been made aware that no word, no gesture, however meaningful and good intentioned, would alter an attitude which seemed determined and destined to lead them on to a path that neither would foresee, but would take them to a point that would be irreversible.

Roy, upon reaching home, and wishing to avoid any such crisis overtaking him and Helen, went up to her to assist her with her coat.

"I can manage, thank you," was her response to his gesture of reconciliation, and she pushed him aside as though the very thought of touching her was repulsive.

He chose to ignore her remark and although he made no further attempt, he did make another gesture which he thought might appease her. "I'll make some coffee. Would you like something to eat as well? A little snack, perhaps?"

"No, thank you!"

"Helen, look…" he began, but she made an impatient and dismissive gesture of the hand, then strode briskly out of the room and into the bedroom and slammed shut the door.

Roy threw himself into a chair and stared dejectedly at his feet. It occurred to him that Helen had sought deliberately to provoke a crisis. Her behaviour was meant to have one purpose, yet even though he was aware of that now, he could not bring himself to admit to what seemed inevitable.

Waving his arms in a gesture of baffled resignation he rose and strode out of the room and into the kitchen.

Chapter five

"Come on now, get out. You heard me? Get out of here this minute! Go into the next room and play."

Mayfield, having chased the children away, closed the door after him, seated himself in an armchair and stretched out his sandaled feet. "Can't get peace in this house you know, when these are around." He listened a moment for sounds from the room into which he had sent the children, then, satisfied that all was well in there, he cast a brief glance about him and turned to look at Helen. "Well, you look alright" he said after an approving contemplation of her appearance. "Yes, I must say you're looking well." He smiled now. "Must be enjoying life, no doubt."

Helen sat opposite to him, her legs stretched out, her hands folded in her lap as was her custom, her father silently noted. Almost as though she was expecting anything with no surprises whatsoever. She had that way of staring straight at one, with a twitch of the nose as if any moment she were going to laugh, or wanted one to laugh.

She did not look at her father now, but stared alternatively at her hands and at the floor. Mayfield sensed that something was wrong. For several weeks now the incident in the street had rankled within her. Then there had been other occasions as well when she had deliberately sought a quarrel with Roy, over minor, inconsequential things. Sometimes she wondered what was happening to her, why she seemed forever so eager to take issue with Roy, even when he tried to assist her with her studies. Unable to define her new self she had thought of talking to someone about her dilemma. She had had a busy time in making up her mind about coming to her father. He seemed to her, when she gave the matter some thought, that he would be the one person, the only person it would be best in whom to confide. A smile played on her lips. Isn't it ironical, though, she thought. Him, who had never cared much about her.

She hesitated a moment, shifting her feet uncomfortably from one position to the other. "I....I want to tell you about something," she began.

"I thought as much," her father said, looking straight at her, then added petulantly, "You only come to see me when you need me, when you are in some trouble. Well....that's alright. I'm your father and I suppose that is what I am here for."

Helen repressed a strong inclination to laugh. She looked pointedly at her father for a moment, then, lowering her head to look at her feet, could not help chuckling. "It's a bit late, ain't it" she observed with an edge to her voice that had the effect of temporarily cutting the ground from under her father's feet. "Rather late to remind me of that, don't you think?"

Mayfield thought it better to ignore that remark. "Alright, but you don't have to reproach your father now, you know" he answered her in all penitence. His wife came in then and he turned to face her. She gave no indication that she wished to be brought into the conversation and remained silent, leafing through the pages of the newspaper, 'The West Indian World.' "Well, alright," Mayfield resumed. "What's the matter, then? What's happened?" He turned again to his wife. "Anita, dear, make us some tea, will you?"

"Yes, alright"

"Well," Mayfield said as soon as his wife had left the room. "What has happened now?"

"Oh, I don't know," Helen said, and shrugged vaguely, uncertain now whether or not to go on with what she had come to tell him. "I just don't know."

"Are you not happy with Roy, then?

"Oh, he's alright" she told him, yet her countenance revealed a profound predicament. "There's no one else in the whole wide world I would prefer to have married. None. I look about me and I think of all those fellers I used to know, used to think about like crazy. Yeah! But now? Now I feel sick just to think that at one time I had ever thought of marrying anyone of them. A bunch of morons! No more than that. No ambition except to listen to Reggae music all day long, discos at week-ends. No ideas whatever. No nothing! Just filling in the time between birth and death, that's all. That's what it is, really." She paused a moment, then continued "No, I could not have asked for a better husband. But I am not comfortable in my mind, and that's what's causing all the trouble. That's what's making me so unhappy. I know I shouldn't be, but that's how I feel."

Her father considered this in silence for a moment. He looked at her and noted once again how elegantly dressed she was sitting there, and the thought came to him that he had never before seen her looking so pretty, so tidy, and so healthy in appearance, and he knew that he had never been able to get her to look half so contented as she appeared to be. He shook his head, puzzled. Could he be wrong? She said she was unhappy, but what was the cause?

He asked again, without thinking "What's the matter, then? Tell me, Helen."

"Oh, I don't know, dad. I mean….he's good to me, right? He'll do anything for me; I know that. Maybe he even loves me, I don't know. Don't laugh, dad. Perhaps I don't really understand what love is. Come to think of it, I cannot ever remember seeing anything like 'love' in our house when I was growing up. But…"again she gestured vaguely, helplessly, and looked across at her father, and her large hazel eyes seemed to appeal for sympathy, for some understanding of her predicament. "What is it, I don't know."

"So, what has happened?" Mayfield asked after a moment's further reflection during which neither father nor daughter understood nor saw a solution to the dilemma. Mayfield's head was bowed, but now he looked up at Helen and asked "You don't feel that you love him, then? Is that what it is?"

"Oh, I like him very much. I do. I have the greatest respect for him….the greatest respect. I admire him. He's bright; he's good and kind…." Her voice trailed off, growing softer and more distant.

Mayfield could not restrain a gesture of utter confusion. He realized in an instant of sad reflection that he did not really know his daughter. He said now "Then…if he's so good to you….why are you unhappy? I don't understand at all."

The question did not help at all and Helen felt even greater distress now. She knew that she had to find an answer, a solution, somehow. She had relied upon her father to assist her to find one, otherwise she would be lost. She had come to talk to him about her problems, she reflected now. And had been prepared to tell him all in return for help.

"His standards are too high for me" she said now. "You have no idea how far apart our two worlds are, him and me. The way he was brought up, the things they did at school; his childhood back home; the games he played. I went to school in this country and didn't have those opportunities. No one at school cared about us black girls and boys. I didn't even start to understand the English language thoroughly until I married the man. They had drilled it into us that grammar was not important, and when we didn't get good jobs we didn't know why; or we thought the wrong reasons. Only now does anything make sense. I realize now that I hardly knew anything. I had had to fight for the little education that I have, otherwise I would never have had those G.C.Es that I managed to get. You know something? I listen to those boys and girls talk, his friends, and I have to keep quiet most of the time. Can you imagine me keeping quiet during a discussion? I listen and am scared stiff to open my mouth. They make me feel so small just with one sentence."

She laughed out of embarrassment and looked appealingly at her father. She shook her head in a gesture of self-pity as though the very thought of her discovery had shamed her beyond bearing. "It's humiliating, you know," she said. "To think that my own father and mother did not even bother to take an interest in my education, or in me having a decent upbringing if nothing else." She chuckled to herself. "When these boys and girls were going to college I had to be going out to work, doing menial jobs, or I had to remain at home to mind the youngest children. What kind of a life was that? Eh? Tell me. When I should have been at school I was being tossed from one to the other of you like a rubber ball; without a proper home; sometimes without anything to eat all day. I don't know why I'm telling you all this now because you know all about it. All I can say after all that is that I feel like an intruder, an upstart. Not at all like a wife. And what troubles me night and day is that I cannot get it out of my mind that Roy knows it. So do his friends, I'm sure. And it makes me feel awful! Just bloody awful, I tell you!"

Her father had turned away from her a while, listening to her, and now he moved uneasily in his chair. He stared at his feet, then at his hands, and finally turned again to look at her. His eyes were watery now and there was an air of supplication in his gesture when he tried to speak, but no words came. He gave up, waving his hands in a final gesture of despair. What, indeed, he asked himself, was there for him to say in his own defence? Nothing.

Helen laughed now, irreverently, recalling something from long ago. "You remember how bad my English used to be when I started seriously to study for my exams? I could speak the thing well enough, but when I came to write it I didn't have a clue! At first I used to ask the teacher for the meaning of words, or how to spell them and she would smile at me. I didn't understand the meaning of those smiles. Then I used to be embarrassed and come to you. What's a verb? A transitive one? An irregular verb. I remember the look on your face. What's a subordinate clause?"

Mayfield thought of saying something, but decided against it. He felt cornered.

"You remember what you used to tell me? That I shouldn't worry about such things. Not important, you said. to me. Not important? Christ! You were no better than those damned white teachers. I had to fight for my education. Once I discovered those things, and other things as well were important, I practically had to tutor myself."

Her father felt that she was exaggerating somewhat and he smiled indulgently. "Well, you've got on so far, my dear. So you see? Why do you have to worry about all those things now?"

Helen looked over at him and wondered about his stupidity. How could he be so complacent? Simply because one belonged to another class in the society, she told herself, one did not have to remain ignorant, uneducated and incompetent, relegated to that section of the population that furnished only the servile ones. She had detected that attitude in the British working class, and she refused to accept it; to accept permanently that place decreed by the "others." No. She would never accept what "they" wanted to force her and her people to accept. She refused to accept, also, that what "they" thought was good enough for her parents was good enough for her.

"So, you see, dad, it does matter. I discovered that long ago. And being married to Roy has confirmed it. I don't even feel like going to him to ask him anything now. I feel so embarrassed."

"You should never feel embarrassed to talk to your husband, or to ask him anything."

She cast a glance at him full of pity. "Dad", she said quietly and slowly, for she felt somehow that she had to bring him to the reality of the particularly humiliating situation in which she found herself, "you and my mother should have seen to that years ago, instead of thinking only about yourselves all the time."

Her father waved his hands in a brief gesture of dismissal, but too feeble to demolish Helen's discomforting exposure of the neglect of his duties.

Helen pressed home her points. "I only have to ask Roy or one of his friends one simple question and they go into such detailed explanations that I get smaller and smaller. You would never have imagined that I had gone to school, and in this England at that! I feel like an intruder, I tell you. Honestly. I feel I don't belong in that company. And I can't....I can't live with that thought haunting me day and night. And it's all your blasted fault! You and that blasted mother of mine. You all brought me into this country. Why? Not even you could have afforded to do the things that Roy is doing for me. Why didn't you all care for us? I know what's possible now, thanks to Roy. But I would have felt better if you had told me years ago, put me on the right track. A stranger had to come to do that....even though he is my husband."

She began to cry, and her father rose to put his arms about her shoulders to console her. "Don't let that upset you, Helen. Don't...."

"Well, it bloody well has upset me!" Helen screamed at him. "And it makes me feel all the time like a bloody fool, because I can't help feeling that he's doing me a favour and that he knows it."

Mayfield walked to the door through which his wife had disappeared earlier and, as though by some pre-arranged signal, knocked upon the door. His wife came out with the tea and stood for a moment in indecision. Then she placed the tray on the table and looked questioningly at her husband. Mayfield gestured towards Helen.

"Pour her out a cup, please," he said, then he turned to look at Helen. "Drink it. dear. It will do you good."

"I don't want any, thank you."

"Come on, Helen." Mayfield pursued in a tone of voice which carried the semblance of severity which he had not intended. Immediately he regretted it. He softened instantly. "Drink it, my dear. Please drink some. It will help steady your nerves and you'll feel better for it."

"I said I didn't want any!" She had raised her voice imperiously as though she were dealing with a recalcitrant child. "Why won't you all understand how I feel? "

"Alright, alright," Mayfield said quickly and with a gesture that at once conceded defeat and resignation. "If you don't want it, it's alright. We're not forcing you."

Helen continued to sob and they let her cry. After a while she stopped, then fetched a handkerchief from her handbag to dry her eyes and to blow her nose. She replaced the handkerchief and regarded the handbag with an ironical smile.

"You know," she said, speaking softly as though remembering an event that ought not to have been. "This is the first real leather handbag that I've ever possessed. And that coat hanging there, he bought for me also. This dress and these shoes, too. I never thought these mattered because you and my mother never did anything decent like that for me. What did you all ever do but try to ruin our lives. You all made me what I am by not caring. A no-good, useless good-for-nothing, that's what I feel like. And you, "she turned to face Anita, "because my mother is not here anymore you, too, are responsible." She looked at Mayfield now and continued "You call yourself my father!" Of a sudden she leapt to her feet, hurriedly put on her coat and, snatching up her handbag, exclaimed in a voice charged with anger, mortification and utter dejection "Let me get out of this place before I go mad and do something stupid! Mad! Mad! Mad!"

She went to the door, opened it and shut it behind her with such violence that the very house seemed to vibrate with the shock.

"Jesus Christ!" Anita blurted out. "She is in a bad temper, isn't she?"

Mayfield did not answer. He remained staring at the floor for a long time deep in thought, clasping and unclasping his hands. He recalled his own childhood, one of a broken marriage as well, when neither his mother nor his father had wanted him after their divorce. His maternal grandmother and finally his aunt on his father's side, had taken it in turns to look after him. He had grown up hard, independent, cynical. Whatever education he had received was what he had acquired back home, which was not much, considering the circumstances of his disrupted childhood. Selfish, he was, also, and he did not try to conceal it.

"She's right, you know," he said after a while, more to himself than to his wife who stood a little away from him and close to the door of the kitchen. "She's quite right. I should have looked after her, after all of them, but I didn't. I should have brought her up properly. A boy is different. He can take life as it comes, look after himself. A girl? Well, a girl.....With a girl it's harder. Too many distractions in this city, and you soon forget what's right and what's wrong. What's good and what's bad. And this country doesn't help; doesn't care. If anything, it encourages you to go the wrong road, and then they tell you they can help you. It's difficult for a girl, that's true. More destructive. She's right. It's all my fault. We have no business bringing children into this world if we know we can't or won't be able to look after them properly. No business at all."

His wife did not say anything to that. She knew that she was not supposed to say anything whenever Mayfield was in that frame of mind. He sat himself down after delivering himself of that confession, and now he got up again to put on his shoes and his overcoat.

"Where are you off to now?" his wife felt prudent to ask. "It's cold outside. You're not going after her, are you?"

"No. I'm only going round the corner."

She understood how he felt and where he had to go to drown his sorrows. "Well, don't overdo it. Take care of yourself, you hear?" She gave him the briefest of glances as he paused at the door, and in her eyes he read all the sympathy and understanding that she felt for him. She smiled at him, a smile that revealed more than she could convey in words.

"She'll leave him, you know" Mayfield said. "She cannot bring herself to be grateful to him for what I should have done for her."

Anita understood that she was not expected to say anything to that either.

Mayfield closed the door quietly as he went out.

Chapter six

Roy made his way from the bus stop in the Strand and crossed over to the other side by the huge and elegant Courts Bank. The Queen's bank, he had been told. He walked up the short street to the Post Office in Trafalgar Square and noticed the name of a street ahead of him, Chandos Street. The name struck a note. He recalled reading something about someone by that name. It was a man and there had been a great deal of controversy about him. The writer had called him one of the most wicked men who had ever lived. He hated Blacks. Roy remembered then that it had to do with the British Government and....Where was it now? Oh, yes! Africa. Lord Chandos, one-time Colonial Secretary at the time of the Kikuyu people's fight for their freedom from British rule. Lyttleton, that was the man's original name before he was made Lord Chandos.

Roy shook his head. History! British colonial history was like a haunted tomb. You wanted to forget the experience of that encounter, but the memories attached themselves to you and you could neither escape nor forget that past. It haunted you down through the centuries.

He had entered the building, but he walked through and over to the far end and out on to the pavement to look at Nelson's statue with thought of history still bedeviling him. Nelson, the Battle of Trafalgar, the Battle of the Saints in the Eastern Caribbean, 1782. He gazed at the statue for a long time before returning inside to buy an air letter.

He was standing at the long counter, writing, when two old tramps, one black, the other white, came in and stood talking a little way from where Roy was standing. They did not come for anything but merely to shelter from the cold outside. They must have been in discussion before coming in and came in to continue. Roy paid scant attention to them until he heard them disagreeing about some detail of Latin grammar. Roy stopped writing to look at the two disheveled old men, almost in rags, and was amazed at what he was hearing. Two tramps discussing Cicero's 'Pro Milone.'

He smiled, he did not know why, but of a sudden it occurred to him that those two must have had a good education in the distant past, but had never forgotten what they had learnt. Fate, he thought now as he continued to look at the two tramps, plays some tricks on people. Perhaps those two might even have been teachers in their time. Now in their old age they were walking the streets aimlessly, perhaps even sleeping it rough beneath one of the London bridges where he, Roy, had often seen them gather for the night.

Roy shook his head in amazement. One never knows what one will encounter in life. He was still engrossed in those thoughts and about to complete his letter when he heard a male voice, and then a hand tapping him gently on the shoulder.

"What's happening, man?"

Roy spun around to the left, out of habit, a tip he had learned long ago from a film, never to turn in the direction of the hand tapping the shoulder. "Delgado, man! What's happening? Haven't seen you in months."

"Almost eighteen months" Delgado said, and laughed his loud, gruff laughter. "Not since some time after your wedding."

He was a man with a large frame, a little tall and already going bald, although he was only in his early thirties. He was always neatly dressed which gave him a somewhat distinguished appearance. Debonair, really.

"That's right," Roy said in confirmation. "A long time ago, man. Where have you been hiding. No one can contact you anywhere."

"Been traveling" he said, and laughed again. "The continent. You're in a hurry? Okay, wait for me, non. I won't be long."

Delgado came from Grenada and had come to study medicine, but had given that up and had taken up analytical chemistry and now he was finished and had graduated. From time to time he vanished from his regular haunts, a coffee bar in South Kensington and a night club in the basement of a church in the Fulham Road, and no one knew where he went. The coffee bar was run by a very attractive young brunette who had married an homosexual, a strange combination, Roy had always thought. The brunette had a lover, a handsome black West Indian actor from Jamaica who spoke with a very English accent.

Whenever Delgado returned from wherever he had been he always had some stirring tales to relate of distant countries where he had been. Even as a student he had had a calling for films and had often been given small parts to play. He enjoyed it, he would tell Roy, both for the money and for the people whom he met on those occasions, especially the young actresses with whom he would have brief affairs. About them he would talk familiarly and with a frank intimacy that had his listeners envious. What a lucky devil, they would exclaim.

Roy sealed the air letter he had been writing and dropped it into the post box. He heard Delgado ask for a postal order for twenty pounds. He tucked the money order into an envelope, then sealed and posted it. He paused just the fraction of second in thoughtful contemplation of the letter box, then turned to face Roy with a smile.

"So, tell me, partner, what's been happening?"

"Nothing much" Roy said, then observed "You look like you hit the pools."

Delgado laughed. "No, man. Just some luck in a poker game last night. Always send something every week to the folks back home. You know what I mean? When the luck is good, especially on the horses, they get an extra helping. Not much time left for them, you know, so I try to make life pleasant and comfortable for them. You know what I mean? Christ only knows how much of a hard time they had bringing me up and paying for my education in this blasted world."

"That's a lot of money to win at a game," Roy said.

Delgado laughed. "That's nothing, man. Some of the big time fellers win and lose thousands of pounds on some nights. I'm a small timer."

They left the post office and decided to walk in the direction of Green Park. They passed a church and Delgado, having seen that there were benches in the churchyard, suggested that they sit awhile beneath one of the trees.

"Let's just sit and watch the world go by" Delgado said. "You're not in a hurry, are you?"

"No. Not really."

"Good. That's the damned troubled with this place. Everybody in a hurry going no-place at all. Crazy, man! Crazy!"

Roy examined him more closely and noted that Delgado had lost some weight. He was, as always elegantly dressed with his neatly trimmed moustache and hair slightly greying at the temples which made him look older than he really was. Roy discovered later that Delgado had purposely dyed the hair grey, for, he divulged, the women in London fell for that sort of thing in a big way. Roy wondered why and Delgado said that it made him look very Spanish, very Latino. He would, also, he said, punctuate his speech occasionally with one or two Spanish phrases. That, too, went down well with the English women, and the film directors. He looked younger now because he had slimmed down a little.

Roy recalled his first encounter with Delgado, the night of the wedding. Delgado had introduced an entirely novel approach to the art of gate-crashing. The door below had been left open and

Delgado, hearing the music, had simply walked in, and with a bold knock had entered.

"Is it here that Mr. Delgado has been invited" he had asked.

The guests had turned to look at Roy, and Helen had smiled and remarked that another of Roy's guests had arrived….late. "Who is he?" she had asked.

"I don't know the man," Roy had whispered. What shall we do?"

Helen had giggled and had said "He's a funny man" and had observed that the man had not even bothered to wait for an answer. "He's already walked in, anyway. Let's leave him alone."

Roy had shrugged, smiling. "Well, let's make him feel at home." Then he had walked over to the newcomer. "Hello, man? How're things?"

"Cool, man. Everything's just cool." He had given Helen and Roy the briefest of glances. "God, partner, this is real fete, man! Look at people! I haven't seen fete like that for a long, long time. Not since that time in St. Georges when the war ended. Boy, is back home we used to have fete. I remember when I was in Port-of-Spain, we used to have some fetes! With all them Yankees in town and rum and dollars flowing like water. Fetes! But those days are gone. Gone, man. Gone."

"Well, have fun" Roy had said to him. "Help yourself to drinks. And there's plenty of food on the table in the next room."

"Right, partner. Right." Then Delgado had leaned over and had asked Roy in a whisper "Listen, man. You look like a real nice test. Whose fete is this? And what's it in aid of? Tell me, non."

Roy had in turn leaned over to him and had whispered the information, as though in confidence. "Well, to tell you the truth, it's my fete, but don't tell anyone, you hear? I got married to-day, and this young lady here is my wife. And my name, by the way, is Roy, and my wife's name is Helen. How do you do?"

Delgado had rocked back on his heels with laughter. "Alright, partner. I feel you, old man! Yes, that's a classic. Dig me some skin, man! "And he had extended his hand. "My name is Delgado. Ex-R.A.F. Corporal. Gunner and all that. How do you do?"

They had shaken hands, laughing.

"Aaaah! That's a fine craft you've married there. Gimme a dance with her, non."

And before Roy had given an answer he had whirled Helen away to the music of a Cadance. He brought her back when the music had ended. "Thanks, pal. See you later" Having taken a handful of cashew nuts he had walked away, saying to Roy "This is fete, man! This is fete's father!"

Helen and Roy had watched him with amusement as he joined a group on the far side of the room. Some time later, passing close to the group, they had heard him protesting to one of the young men who had been an aspiring Calypsonian, The Duke.

"Man, you talking stupidness!"

Everyone turned to look at him which is what, Roy surmised, he had intended. Delgadio, he had later discovered, had a way of compelling attention that was entirely innovative. He would enter any conversation, uninvited, make the wildest and most outrageous of statements, then take over the conversation from there.

"If you want to talk about Calypso, my friend, you must come to me. I come from Grenada and grew up in Trinidad. So you must know what that means." He had looked about him then to ascertain that he had a sufficiently large audience and, satisfied of that, had continued "Man, you want to hear the latest Calypso? Lend me that guitar and let be burst a tune on you. Listen to Calypso, boy. You haven't heard Calypso yet. Since when Jamaicans can sing Calypso? Behave yourself, man! Next thing you'll be telling that penguins make whiskey in the North Pole."

Laughter had vibrated throughout the room. With that Delgado had snatched the guitar from The Duke, strummed a few chords and, surrounded by an eager, expectant crowd, he had first sang a Calypso about politics in modern Britain. Soon he had the crowd about him singing the chorus, a catchy tune, indeed.

Roy had watched him, smiling the while, and had thought how clever Delgado was. It were as though Delgado had been at home once more in Grenada. That was the way it would have been back home, Roy had been thinking. That was the essence of the Calypso; the audience had to be with the Calypsonian from the very first opening lines. And it was in the nature of a Caribbean audience quickly to learn the tune and the lyrics of the chorus.

Delgado had sung several Calypsos that night, some of which were his own composition.

Roy recalled now how the atmosphere had changed that night; how the melodies had filled the room, floated away, transporting them back to the Caribbean. He remembered, also, how he had imagined that he almost felt the warmth of the sun, had heard, or thought that he had heard the distant strumming of the guitar, and the stirring, haunting rhythm of the steel band.

"Kaiso!"

A couple of West Indians passed by, harmonizing.

Delgado turned to look at Roy an asked about his studies. Roy shrugged and it occurred then to Delgado that something was amiss. "Everything alright at home?" he ventured to ask after a moment's reflection.

"Well," Roy began with a gesture which Delgado interpreted as one of resigned perplexity. "There are the good moments and there are the bad."

"That's life, man" Delgado said. "Nothing ever runs smoothly.

"And how is it with you?" Roy asked in turn.

Delgado spread out his hand wide. "As you can see. I'm living. No complaints."

"That's good" Roy said.

There was that in his voice, Delgado thought, that made him cast a quick glance at Roy. He observed his friend's subdued countenance and it occurred to him that Roy must be wrestling with some major problem. Was it his studies? He wondered. He had met Roy occasionally since the night of the wedding and he was not at all pleased to note the decidedly changed demeanor which now revealed itself from that one-time cheerfulness and infectious smile.

Roy gave no indication that he wished to discuss whatever was occupying his mind. Delgado shrugged away his concern and turned his attention to the people who were passing by on their way to the church to listen to an organ recital which he had noticed was advertised on the notice board outside the church. The recital was to begin in half an hour. He cared not overmuch for the church and he kept his ideas and his observations about the priesthood to himself. Sometimes he wondered how long did it take for a religion to become respectable, recalling the stormy passage of time when the adherents of Christianity were forcing their ideas on to other people. Intolerance had been the order of the day, with doubters and unbelievers standing no chance of remaining alive once they had been discovered, or had been reported as heretics. The odour of burning flesh marked the forced arrival of Christianity in Europe, a theology which formed the principal weapon of the European imperialists and colonialists.

Indeed, History is a haunted tomb.

He watched as two women approached and from their features he deduced that they were a mother and her daughter. He tried to guess the young woman's age, about thirty or thirty-five. The mother herself could not have been more than fifty-five.

Of a sudden it came into Delgado's head to divert Roy from whatever was causing him to be so disconsolate. He approached the young woman.

"Lady, can you spare me a cigarette?"

The woman, offended that she had been addressed so unceremoniously, turned her head away, pretended not to have heard and she and her mother hurried their steps.

Roy, embarrassed, wondered what Delgado was up to. He turned to his friend "Look, man, if you want cigarettes I'll get you some."

Delgado laughed. "Sit down and keep quiet, man. Where you're going? Stay where you are and let me have my fun."

"But...Jesus Christ, man!"

Delgado laughed again. "Take it easy, man" he said. "Watch this." With that he walked up to the young woman. :"Lady, have you a cigarette to spare? That's what I asked. And in English, too, so don't tell me you didn't understand me."

The mother looked about her. "How dare you!" she exclaimed and for a moment Roy thought that she would strike Delgado with her furled umbrella.

Delgado looked at her and smiled. "It's alright, lady. I'm talking to your daughter, not to you. I only want a cigarette, that is all. A tu compris?"

The young woman, to Roy's surprise, and to Delgado's amusement which showed by the smile on his face, handed him an entire packet of cigarettes which she extracted from her handbag.

Delgado, still smiling, reminded her politely that he only wanted one cigarette, that was all. "Anyway, thank you all the same. Most generous of you. Hope you enjoy your recital. Wagner is much too heavy for me, the damned fascist. Me, I like the Romantics, Mozart and all that, you know." With that Delgado bowed and turned away, laughing, to rejoin Roy on the bench.

"But, you're a hell of a man, you know! " Roy said to him as Delgado sat down to light his cigarette "Why did you have to do such a thing? And to embarrass me so?"

"Embarrass you? How did I embarrass you?" He inhaled slowly on his cigarette, then let out a long cloud of smoke. "You know something, Roy? For three years I served this country in the Air Force, Sometimes I wonder if it's the same people for whom I fought and nearly lost my life, the way they're treating us now." He laughed a strange, sardonic laugh and let out another long cloud of smoke. "I'll tell you something.

One of my buddies who had fought beside me, also, couldn't get anything to do back home, and like many of us he returned here. He had always fancied joining the Police Force.

"I remember that day well, in May, 1960, when I went to the Police Station with him in the West End. Not far from here. The sergeant, or whatever he was, who was at the desk didn't even raise his head for a long time to attend to us. He pretended he was writing something. I remember his words exactly."

"Yes, what do you want?"

"No politeness in his voice and his manner at all. My friend asked about joining the Police Force. You know what he did? He called to the other policemen in the other room. Called out to them to 'Come and see and hear this. Come and see this monkey who wants to join the Force'"

Delgado paused to laugh, a soft sardonic laugh and took another pull on his cigarette.

"Come and look at this monkey who wants to join the Force. And to-day, you hear them? They want Blacks to join the Force, and they wonder why they're not being too successful. It's not Blacks they want. What they need to do is to change their attitude towards us. Until that is done they'll have trouble getting Blacks to join. A bunch of fascists!"

Roy wondered what had happened to the fellow, He asked Delgado.

"Who? Which fellow?" His mind seemed to have wandered.

"The one who wanted to join the Police Force?"

"Oh, him?" Delgado chuckled. "Man, if I tell you, you won't believe it. He's back in his island home now. He went into politics, and now he's Deputy Prime Minister."

"Well, at least he found his niche. But, I can well understand what his views must be when he hears what's happening to West Indians in this country."

"Can't blame him." Delgado said. "Can't blame him at all. And after fighting a war for them."

He smoked in silence for a while and from time to time Roy looked at him, but said nothing. He saw the smile that played on Delgado's lips, as though he was enjoying some private joke.

Presently Delgado said, as though talking to himself "We had no business in that war. It was a European affair, cousin to cousin business. I see that clearly now. Now that's it's all over they're hugging and kissing each other as though nothing had aver happened between them. And you see what's happening? They're all laughing at us all over the place. They're banding together and ganging up against us. This is a crazy world, man. And it serves us right."

Now that he had offered some explanation for is behaviour Roy was less critical and even felt a tinge of sympathy for his friend. There were occasions, he recalled now, because he knew that he was in the country for a short period only, when he sometimes felt that what was going on, what was happening to black people did not really affect him unduly. He tried to convince himself that it was none of his concern. Until he met Delgado he tended to regard the West Indians who had settled in England as a lost tribe. They had chosen to make their contributions in another country. Very well. Through no fault of their own. What had the islands to offer them, anyway? One had to remember that. Some might be ambitious and will make something of their lives, hopefully.

He heard Delgado let out a chuckle and he turned to look at him. "No, no business at all," Delgado repeated to himself.

Now that he was convinced that his friend had not taken leave of his senses in approaching the women in the manner that he had done, Roy felt something of sympathy for him. He felt bold enough to say so.

Delgado merely laughed. We have all to face up to life was the view he expressed, because that's how life happens to be, made up of individuals. No one could honestly tell another how to lead his life. Life? One faced life alone, most of the time. One made a success or a mess of it depending upon the way one chose to live one's life. If that had not been so the one philosophy would have been sufficient for the entire world. But the very fact that the world had produced so many philosophers throughout history proved his point. From Plato, Aristotle, Christ, Rousseau, Kant, Marx down to Sartre…they all preached the same thing each in his different way…How to live; how to cope with life. All of them critical of life as it was lived in their day; all of them offering advice, making suggestions. Yet we are still here with the same problems, perhaps seeming magnified because they appear on a much larger scale, and global, because technology has made communication and the movement of information much easier and faster.

But we still have to answer the most fundamental of questions in the universe…What is life? What is the purpose of life? So many of us do not even try to understand why we are here. Delgado chuckled. There is a fellow in a volume of poetry 'Palgrave's Golden Treasury,' Omar Khayyam. He was a mathematician, an astrologer and a poet. Sometime in the twelve century, if his memory did not deceive him, Delgado was saying. Hell and Paradise were right here on earth, was Khayyam's conclusion. He preached that life was a meaningless game. Other people, philosophers and religious people, have had different ideas.

"Look at that woman who gave me the cigarettes." Delgado continued a moment later after exhaling cigarette smoke and a pause for reflection. "At her age still a virgin. I could tell from the shape of her backside and by the way she walked, keeping her legs close together. She has never known a man in her life. She trembled when she handed me the pack of cigarettes. Not out of fright because I was not about to mug her. Nor was I going to rape her....would have been a waste of time and energy, anyway; they're so cold anyway when you're making love to them. Not like a black woman who's like a tornado under you. She trembled because she was nervous at having a man speak to her. And in an authoritative manner, too. I can imagine how boring life must be for her. I can well understand that. Living somewhere in the suburbs in her detached house, hardly speaking to the neighbours. Watching life go by peeping behind curtains which she would open just slightly. I must have done her a big favour, the most exciting thing that has ever happened in her life. To-night she will go to sleep and even dream about the incident. Maybe she might even have an orgasm in her sleep, poor thing. She'll have something to talk about from to-day onwards. Instead of the usual dreary and desultory subjects of the weather and what was on television.

"Why do you think I did what I did, eh? To give her some excitement, that's all. To make something happen in her life. Crazy? I'll bet you thought I was? No, man. Sometimes I do get some fantastic ideas, I have to admit. Some outlandish thing that enters my head. Like wanting to open up these people to see if they have any blood, if they're human. I think that's why they were able to conquer and rule almost half the world. They have no humanity.

"Really crazy ideas, I tell you. Like you know, after the Christine-John Profumo affair. You don't know about that? Well, some day I'll tell you all about it. Well, after that scandal I would sometimes take it into my head just to go up to a young woman and address her as though I had been with her the night before. Just for kicks, man, because these people are too hypocritical. They know it is happening all the time. They know that their women can't keep away from the black men, but they pretend it never happens. All the mulattos in this place had been miraculously conceived. That only happ4ned in the Bible, man. Not in to-day's world.

"I'll tell you something that will make you laugh. The other night I took a woman to my place; about forty she is, I should imagine. She had not had a man for oh, hell knows how long ago, she told me afterwards.

Went berserk when I was making love to her. Nothing like that had ever happened to her before she said. Bawled her head off. Crazy! Good thing I live in a basement. The woman got so excited, when I was finished with her my back was like a map showing criss-crossing rivers. What a country, eh? Men fighting to be women and women wanting desperately to be masculine."

Delgado sudden stopped and looked at his watch. "Eh, eh! Here we are, man, only having dry talk. You have time? Let's go home and kill a bottle with me, man."

"Well, so long as I am home by eleven, then that's alright by me."

Helen had gone to visit her father and she had indicated that she would not be back before eleven. He thought it strange that she had taken to visiting her father so frequently of late. He recalled her telling him often enough that she never wanted to see her father again. It had got so that he had resolved to keep away from his father-in-law's home, for he did not wish to be present when that ugly scene would come, according to Helen which was bound to happen one of these days. Better to keep out of this father and daughter clash altogether.

Delgado stopped a passing taxi and directed the driver to an address in Victoria in South West London. When they arrived at their destination Delgado paid the taxi driver and waited until the taxi had disappeared round a corner, then he walked back two blacks to the house where he lived.

"You can never tell who thee chaps are," he explained. "Might be MI6 or CIA, or even crooks. Or more likely police in disguise trying to pin something on you to work out a grudge, to take revenge on whatever they think the Blacks are up to, exposing themselves for what they really are, racists and fascists, same thing. Or very often placing drugs on a Black and taking him in. Don't laugh. It happens often enough."

Roy thought that Delgado had misinterpreted the smile on his face. Not that he had not taken Delgado's observations and precautions seriously. He had read enough about such things in the papers, and had heard some of the West Indians and Africans at the university talk about such things happening to someone whom they knew.

He followed Delgado down into the basement. It was the first time that he had ever been to the apartment and he looked about him as he walked down the short flight of steps to the door which Delgado now opened.

The kitchen was to the left directly beneath the pavement. There was no outlet save the entrance to the kitchen. It must have been, formerly, a coal cellar for he observed the covered outlet for the coals when the coalman used to empty the sacks of coals from the pavement. He had a vision of coal fires and a smog-enveloped London such as he had read about in the novels by Charles Dickens, or had seen in films about the London of those days.

Something else struck him as peculiar, the absence of light in the rooms into which Delgado had taken him to show him. One window faced the street, but because passers-by would have been able to look directly into the sitting room, the curtains were always kept closed. The bedroom, also, contained only one window and that looked out onto another building some two yards away. No light could ever penetrate the bedroom.

Roy thought it a somewhat depressing abode for a West Indian. All that sun and light and outdoor living to which they had been accustomed at home, and now this. What concerned him even more was security. He did not fancy himself living in such conditions. There was no escape except through the front door upstairs if Delgado had to make a quick getaway for whatever reason.

The rooms were tastily decorated, even though it bore all the marks of the abode of a bachelor. There were four small paintings on the walls of the sitting room. The figures were delicately sketched, tall; slim hunters, dancers and drummers, with tall conical headgear like the masqueraders which Roy remembered of some islands in the Caribbean. Roy expected the figures to leap out of the paintings at any moment. He asked Delgado where he had obtained them.

"In the Camerouns. I have a cousin there who is working as a magistrate. I spent some time there with him a couple of years ago. Quite an experience, really. Man, you should see those young women in that country, especially in those remote villages in the hinterland. You never really appreciate what pure beauty is like until you encounter those girls in their natural village surroundings."

"I didn't know that you had visited Africa."

"I've done a bit of traveling, you know. Five years ago I attended a conference in Nairobi. That was my introduction to Africa, the first time I had ever set foot on African soil. But although it was a strange feeling, I did not feel quite emotional about it as I had imagined that I would be. I think it was partly because our people did not come from that part. But I believe what was principally responsible for that non-event was the fact that the damned place was so much like Europe, the big cities, I mean. And the highways. The signs also reminded me of Europe, driving along the motorways. Sometimes I used to wonder where the hell I was! Kenya, Rhodesia, South Africa, they're all the same."

Roy had read something of the events in Africa. Like a large number of West Indians, not only the Rastafarians, Africa was never far from the consciousness of the West Indians.

'That's because they had set out to make those countries a little part of England in Africa" Roy said. They chose the places that suited them best as far as the climate and the possibilities of immense wealth were concerned. Can't blame them when once you've experienced the climate in this country."

Delgado agreed. "Especially when you get four seasons in one day." And he laughed.

Roy wondered if there were anything ever to upset Delgado, any time when he did not laugh. Nothing seemed to bother him unduly. When he returned with a bottle, whiskey this time and two bottles of ginger ale and glasses which he placed on a small table in the centre of the room, Roy asked him about that.

"Well, if I have any problems I don't let it affect anyone else." He laughed. "Who is without problems, anyway? It's how you deal with them that counts. I never let them get me down."

"I wish more people were like you."

"The world would be a very dull place, then" Delgado said, sipping the drink he had poured out for himself.

Roy chuckled. He had noticed the bookshelves along the wall facing the window and he walked over to examine the titles. Delgado informed him that they had been several years of erratic buying, but it occurred to Roy that Delgado had certainly discriminated in favour of history and philosophy. There were also works by some black writers whose names Roy recognized.

He returned to settle down in one of the armchairs and immediately he had the feeling of being at home. He smiled to himself. Only a West Indian home could generate such an atmosphere, he thought to himself, The homes of some of the English students to which he had been invited were distant and cold, and he always had the feeling of wanting to leave immediately he had entered.

"Would you like some tea?" he would be asked. Seldom the offer of a drink. When they offered a drink it was poured out so mean and half an hour later or more he would be asked whether he would like another glass, if he were lucky, that is.

"I see you're interested in philosophy" Roy observed with a nod in the direction of the bookshelves. Some of the titles he had heard of from a friend, Elton, who often spoke about them. But Bardyaev, Heidegger and one thick volume which Delgado had on the table, *The Decline of the West*, by a German named Oswald Spengler.

Delgado smiled and asked whether he had read any of the books and Roy shook his head. He had not the time, he said.

"But there's a pal of mine, a really brilliant fellow, who's always talking about the subject. Those writers you have there, I've heard him mention some of them....Kierkegaard, Nietzsche, Sartre and Jaspers."

"Your friend must be interested in Existentialism. Jaspers is one of them, one of the Existentialist philosophers."

Roy confessed that he knew nothing about such things.

"Strange," Delgado said, "but that's right up your street, literature."

"No, not philosophy."

"You should have been here in the fifties and sixties. We had a wonderful time then, traveling through France, Italy, Spain and Scandinavia. We were interested in things of the intellect in those days. We used to discuss history, philosophy, literature, music, art. Oh, man! It was great in those days! We met on equal terms, white and black. Once during a stay in Paris we met some Russian students. There was a girl who introduced me to Maxim Gorky and Pushkin, Russian writers, and one writer named Gogol." Delgado gazed ahead of him, and his eyes had that distant look of reminiscent pleasure. Then he shook his head and there was a different look in his countenance, one of sadness and regret. "Now it's all about Race, Race, Race!" he said. "And police harassment, that's all you hear and read about in the papers." He threw up a hand in disgust. "Ah! Everything has gone crazy in this place. You would never imagine it's the same place, the same country we fought for. Everything has turned 'ole mas,' man. They've created a new breed of Blacks and made them impotent."

"You mean the ones born here?"

"The ones born here, yes. And those who came here very young and who don't even remember the Caribbean. They have no place to go, no identity. This is the only country, the only life they know."

"You mean things have changed so much? That things were really different in your time?"

"Oh, yes. There was not all that accent on Race and race hatred." He pointed to a volume on one of the shelves, but did not get up to take it down. "That small volume on the second shelf, Nietzsche. He was the one who started it all in a big way. He was the one Hitler embraced. Nietzsche preached the doctrine of the master race, the chosen race. But the man really responsible for the introduction of Race in history was Moses in the

Bible. Moses preached the same thing, that God had chosen the Jews to be the Master Race. 'For thou art an holy people with the Lord thy God. The Lord thy God hath chosen thee to be a special people unto himself, above all people that are upon the face of the earth.' Well, if that isn't a dangerous doctrine, then I don't know what is. I have a theory that that is why the Jews are so hated and persecuted in certain countries. The worse offender was Hitler. He certainly made a mess of the Jews. Their extermination, he thought, was the final solution to what he saw as the Jewish problem. Hitler was one crazy bastard!"

"I find the Jews a most interesting people," Roy said. "I have some in my class. Powerful intellect."

Delgado laughed. "They gave to the world both Christianity and Communism, the two doctrines in which the world is engulfed at present."

"Yes, you're right there" Roy said as though this had never occurred to him before.

"That's why the two are so very similar in their view of History." Delgado said, and chuckled. He got up to go to the kitchen and returned with a bottle, whiskey this time and two bottles of ginger ale.

Roy helped with the opening of the bottles of ginger ale.

"Help yourself, you know" Delgado said. "This is not an English fete" and he chuckled again.

Roy laughed.

"Man," Delgado said "it's good to have a friend drop in now and then like this. You know what I mean? Sometimes I remain in here for days and days and don't go out at all. Do all my shopping on Friday and lock myself in from Friday and read and read and listen to my records. I have a large selection here, you know. Nothing like good music to keep you company. You know want I mean?"

Roy found that odd. He had fancied Delgado to be one who sought always for company and for fun. "But," he hinted in enquiry, "you must wish for company in those moments, non? I suspect you have a woman somewhere to visit you. A man must be a man."

Roy laughed and Delgado joined in the laughter.

He had no special woman, he thought to confide in Roy. "But, as you say, a man must be a man. Oh, I catch a little piece now and then, because this place is a paradise for women. You know what I mean? Next to a London Transport bus, a woman is the easiest thing to catch in this place."

"I have a friend," Roy said, "who always says the same thing."

"An African?"

"No, a fellow from Saint Lucia, A chap named Boze." He told Delgado about Boze, but Delgado had never met him, nor had heard of him.

"We move in different circles," Delgado said. "This place is so large, you can't meet everybody. But, the chap upstairs, he's African. "Man, I've never seen a man who is so lucky and who likes women so! He has a band playing in one of them posh nightclubs in the West End...Mayfair, he told me. Must be a crazy set-up because he comes home most nights with two or three women and it's bacchanal upstairs. I must say this about him, though, he's very discreet. Very. Oh, yes. And that's just what the English women like, discretion. You'll get all the strokes you want, but when you meet them in the street or anywhere, you don't know them, and they don't know you. Everybody's happy, then."

"Crazy!" Roy said.

"Yeah, right. You get the picture."

"They come for their kicks, eh?"

"Right again!" Delgado said.

"What a hell of a world, eh?"

"I didn't make it," Delgado said, and laughed. "I found it so, man. But that don't mean to say I must not enjoy it."

"He must watch out, though, "Roy said. "He must be careful."

Delgado nodded his head, then raised his glass in a gesture of disapprobation and pursed his lips. "One thing....I've warned him already. I've told him that not because women are so free and easy to get here that he must prostitute himself. You know what I mean? Have your women by all means, for your health, but draw the line when they want you only as a stud. But, fellows like him think that their freedom lies between the legs of a woman."

Roy shook his head in distaste at the expression, but managed a smile nevertheless. Delgado got up to select some records and from the bedroom he brought out a portable record player shaped like a grand piano. The voice of The Mighty Sparrow soon filled the room. Roy had heard some of the songs; he hummed them, then joined in the chorus. Delgado then put on the latest by the Mighty Sparrow and which Roy had heard before and he listened as Delgado sang along with Sparrow.

"You have a good voice" Roy said. "Do you sing anywhere?" he thought to ask.

Delgado laughed. "No, man." He had tried, but it seemed he had not the right qualifications. He winked as he said his. "I'm a full blooded male." At that he winked again at Roy and raised his glass.

"I've heard some chaps say that, for the girls, if they want to get on big, they have to serve as the white man's mattress. Is that true?"

"Well, yes, those who don't mind, and are desperate."

"I've been told, also, that this place did not have much entertainment when the West Indians first began to arrive here."

"Yes, that's true. Most of the night clubs were run by our boys. In Soho, Piccadilly, Mayfair. And in a little narrow street off Green Park. Le Contemperain, that one was called. Played mostly Latin music. That used to be fun. Mostly the girls came from the continent, France, Italy, Spain, Sweden and Finland. They were here as au pair girls. On their nights off they came to that club to meet our boys. Those English girls couldn't dance our stuff. They still can't do those things despite trying to copy us. When they dance it's like animals in the last throes of death. Just before the last breath. You know what I mean? Is the same way they make love."

Roy could not restrain his laughter. He had to admit, he said, that Delgado was a good actor, a very excellent comic. "Really good, man." Then he got up and said to Delgado "I must have another drink on that. Yeah, man, you're something else."

They sat drinking and laughing when they heard the doorbell ring.

"That's your doorbell " Roy said.

"Yes, I know." Delgado got up to pull aside the curtain to look out. "Ah, two young ladies have come to see me" he said and winked at Roy.

Roy got up from the chair. "Well, I better be on my way now. It's getting late, a quarter past ten."

"Is it, by Jove? Talking away there time passes quickly, eh?"

Roy accompanied him to the door. "See you again soon," he said. "And, thanks for the drink. It was really pleasant being here."

"Thanks nothing, man. It was great having you here."

Delgado opened the door to welcome his visitors.

Roy stood aside and looked at the two young black women.

"Hello, Ruth. Hello, Assunta," Delgado said. "Meet a friend of mine, Roy "

Roy said "Hello" and shook hands with the two women. "I was just leaving." He looked at the younger of the two. "Ruth, did you say? As in the Bible?"

Ruth smiled, showing teeth that were beautifully white and even.

"They are from South Africa," Delgado told Roy.

"Oh, that's nice" Roy said for want of something better to say, staring unashamedly at Ruth and still holding her hand.

What struck him was the softness of her flesh when he had taken her hand. He still held on to her hand. Her dark velvety complexion stood out against the soft glow of the street light causing her skin to glow a little. He let go of her hand and she stepped aside to allow her to brush pass him and immediately he felt enveloped by the aura of the femininity that she exuded. He smiled at her and she returned his smile.

"Well, see you all sometime" Roy said and regretted that he had to go. Ruth seemed to him to be an interesting person to get to know. He turned to Delgado "I'll drop by again next week. When will you be in?"

"Wednesday. About five. But I have to be out round about nine. Now you know where I live you'll be welcome any time."

Roy walked up the street and onto the pavement. Instinctively he looked first to his left, then to the right. He chuckled as he walked to the Underground Station. Delgado's remarks about caution had already got hold of him without even him thinking about it.

The street appeared deserted and he felt lonely of a sudden. He thought of Ruth, then of Helen. He wondered what was happening between Helen and himself. They were drifting farther and farther apart and now they seemed to be almost strangers. He felt even lonelier now thinking about it.

A train approached as he walked down the steps to the platform and he quickened his steps.

Helen was not at home when he got there. He bathed, made himself a cup of coffee and went to his bedroom to lay down awhile. He dozed off, but just before he fell asleep he had a vision of Ruth. He thought he saw her smiling at him and it was almost as though he could feel, once again, the softness of her hand. Even the scent of her seemed to fill the room inducing sleep.

Chapter seven

Mayfield looked about him angrily, he knew not for what purpose. All day he had spoken but few words to his companions at work, and now Helen had come with more complaints of her own. What was the matter with her? Only last week she had been here…..Or was it this week? He could not even remember. On that morning he had received a letter from his youngest sister, Joyce, who was working in Derby, informing him that she was in the family way for a Welshman who did not want to marry her and, worse, that the man had disappeared.

First Helen, and now Joyce. He had worried over those latest developments all day long. About Joyce he told himself that he could not blame the Welshman. Who would want to marry Joyce, anyway? All fat and lazy as she is? At least the other bloke had had the decency to marry Helen. Now she had come again. He could not understand what was happening to his family.

Helen, on the verge of tears, listened to her father's ranting and bit her lip to stop herself from crying. She watched her father pace the floor as he spoke. Every now and again he would stop to shake his head in despair.

"I don't know," he kept repeating, "I just don't know what is happening." Again he stopped abruptly and turned to face Helen. "So now you want to leave the bloke? Very well. But why did you have to marry him in the first place?"

"You saying that? You saying that now? You seem to forget that it was your idea. It was you who had threatened all sorts of things, you know."

Her father chose to ignore those remarks. "You thought it would be a bed of roses, didn't you? Well, you've found out differently, haven't you? First you and now Joyce." He snorted and Helen repressed the inclination to laugh. "Joyce. Of all the nice black lads of her age and who went to school with her. She had to get mixed up with a white fellow."

He did not see Helen's sarcastic smile. This coming from her father who used to preach such racial tolerance. Who never wanted to hear about White and Black. We are all God's creatures and all that sort of thing.

She said "I didn't expect that from you. What has happened to all those socialist principles of equality of races and all that? It is convenient for you to forget now, eh?"

She thought to tease him some more, but then wondered what would be the use.

"What has happened?" he asked. "What has happened between the two of you?"

She looked at him and shook her head. "Oh, never mind" she said with a gesture of the hands that suggested how hopeless was the matter. "Never mind. It doesn't matter."

Mayfield let out a grunt of satisfaction. It occurred to him that he was still able to inspire fear in her. Well, what if it had been his idea to make the fellow marry her? It had been the easiest way out of a dilemma. Now....it was better to leave him since there were no children to complicate matters. He smiled to himself. He had never fancied those university blokes anyway. He wondered whether it was jealousy. University education! What one wanted was experience. That's what mattered. Experience of life.

Helen continued to look at her father. It had come to her of a sudden that it would be better to leave unuttered what she had intended to say. She did not wish now to create more difficulties for herself. She wanted her father to be on her side for whatever she would make up her mind to do. So she chose silence as the better course. Silence could be interpreted in many ways, and her father had already decided upon only one interpretation, and that suited her purpose.

Mayfield picked up a small chisel with which he had been working on some object and, resuming his pacing of the room, he tossed the instrument into the air, caught it expertly by the handle, tossed it up again, then let it rest in the palm of his hand for a few seconds. He repeated the action several times, then stopped abruptly to look at Helen.

"Right....so you want to leave him. Right? Of course you can leave him. There's nothing to stop you doing that. Nothing in the world. The only thing is that you will have no claim on him once you do that. You understand? Right, then."

Helen continued to remain silent and allowed her father to speak his mind. Yes, it would be better that way. She could no longer have Roy do everything for her. She would have to learn from now on how to stand on her own feet. He had already shown her the way without even being aware of what he had done. God! If only she had been put along the right path years ago, to-day she would not have found herself in this mess. She would try to get a grant to keep her through school for the next year.

Roy had asked her why her father had not helped her to obtain a grant for her before, but she dared not tell him that her father did not care. All he ever wanted was for her to get out and to get a job. Funny that. She would have been well on her way to obtaining a career or a profession had someone pushed her in that direction; someone who cared. Didn't anyone care for her before now?

No, she would not stand for any more of that humiliation. Even to continue to live with Roy now presented a burden such as she could scarcely bear any longer. Already she felt her whole being in revolt. She felt relieved now at the thought that very soon she would be free and would be independent. A wave of determined resolution swept through her. To be on her own again! Only, this time…

"When do you intend to discuss this with him" Or have you already done that?"

She came to with a start out of her reverie. She had lost the thread of whatever he had been saying. She shook her head. "I'll tell him to-night. I've made up my mind about that."

"I see. Well, as I said, you have no children, so that's alright. It makes everything easier. It's better to leave when there are no children. No complications."

She nodded her head, smiling inwardly. Not once, she observed, had he tried to dissuade her from taking such an irrevocable step.

"Of course, as I said, there is nothing that he can do once you've left him. He can ask you to return, but you just ignore that. It would then be up to him to start divorce proceedings. Desertion. That's not so bad, you know. Nothing can happen to you. You always have three quarters of the law on your side. . The worse a judge can do is to deprive you in a case like that, of your children, had you any children Oh, yes. You can leave him any time you like. Anytime."

Again Helen nodded her head. Yes, she had him on her side. Whatever happened from now on she was certain of his support and his protection. That was good. That was all she really wanted.

She wondered about Roy and tried to imagine how he would take the news now that she had come to a decision. She felt she had to tell him, that she owed it to him, for, after all, he had caused her no harm. He only wished good for her. And that was the most difficult part. How could she ever explain; how would he even understand that this very wish of his; those excellent intentions were the very cause of her uneasiness. An uneasiness that had grown and had developed into such proportions as to have become now too burdensome to bear, to tolerate, even, any longer.

Yes, it would be better to tell him, since he could do nothing about her decision, anyway. It would be only fair to tell him. Yet even now, her decision made, some element of doubt remained in her, irritating her, like an unpleasant odour.

"If he attempts any funny business," her father intruded upon her thoughts. "If he attempts any nonsense, don't hesitate to call the police. That'll put him in his place."

Mayfield chuckled at his own cunning and looked over at Helen who sat with her legs wide apart and with her arms dangling between them. She nodded without really grasping the significance of what her father had said. When she rose to go Mayfield walked with her to the bus stop.

"If you ever need any money" Mayfield offered as his parting remark, "I can let you have some. You can pay me back when you start to work."

"Thanks."

On the bus she smiled to herself. Never before had she known her father to be so generous to her. The significance of that did not leave her at all baffled. Throughout the journey her mind became so preoccupied that she missed her stop and had to walk back a block. On the Underground as well she relapsed into such deep thought that she became oblivious to all and everything about her.

She found Roy at the table writing. On the table, also, were a number of books, some opened at particular pages, she observed. Must be writing an essay, she thought. She looked at her watch—the watch which he had given her for Christmas—and discovered that it was almost eleven thirty.

Roy looked up from his writing. "Is everything alright at home?" he asked. "How's your father?"

"He's alright, thank you." And the thought occurred to her, strange, her father had not once asked about him.

"That's good, then." He had imagined that her father was unwell, that was why she visited him so often. But Helen was not forthcoming with any information and he had decided not to pry too deeply. If she wished to confide in him she would do so in her own good time, no doubt.

Roy rose and went into the kitchen where, a moment before, he had put on the kettle for coffee. Helen listened to the sound of his movements and in her mind she rehearsed the words with which she would inform him of her intentions. Her father's advice to summon the police, if necessary, echoed now in her mind like the compulsive strain of some distant melody of which one did not care to have taken any particular attention before.

She called out tentatively "Roy?"

"Yes?"

"Would you mind very much if I left you?"

"What?"

"You heard me. You haven't got cloth ears."

He laughed, loud enough so that she could hear him. It had been a long time since he had heard her use that English expression. He had almost forgotten it. But then she had grown up in this country, had mixed with English boys and girls at school, she would have adopted their manner of speech, sometimes. Strange how time passes, he thought now, and erodes memories. He wondered if life were always like that, as ethereal. Is there not something we can hold on to? Something solid and tangible? Something more solid than memories? There had to be. But each one of us had to discover it for oneself, as Delgado had said. What was his? He had not yet discovered it. That means that the search had to go on, for that something that gives meaning and substance to life...to one's life.

"Well, would you?" Helen asked again.

"What? What have you been drinking at your father's?"

She heard him laugh once more.

"I haven't been drinking anything," she said, and was surprised that she did not feel irritated at all for his not taking her seriously. "But I did ask you a question, though."

"I never answer silly questions, Helen."

"But this is not a silly question, Roy." She could not restrain her laughter, thinking how tragic events invariably have their humorous moments, too. What Roy had called 'comic relief.' "I mean what I asked, Roy."

He brought in the coffee and placed the cups on the table. His manner had about it an air of finality, as though he had already dismissed the subject from his mind and from his consideration, even. She had tried not to be irritated by his manner, but now she felt herself unable to contain herself any longer. So much so that she had to cling to the arm of the chair, so tightly, that she thought she would break it

"Now then," he said and his very tone aggravated her so much that she wanted to throw something at him. Oh, man! You think you're so sure of yourself. Just like a man, isn't it? So blooming well complaisant! Never think that a woman will ever leave him. Chauvinistic, that's what. "Let's have some coffee" he said now. "What do you say to that, eh?"

"Roy." She said and, stifling a scream, she smiled instead to conceal the suppression of the turbulence that threatened to explode any moment. She reminded herself that she must exercise restraint, retain some semblance of calm, at least, for the road upon which she was now embarked would be nothing if not perilous. She told herself that she ought, at least for her own safety, try to uncover, to understand whatever now occupied his mind, so that she would the better deal with any eventuality. "Roy," she said again and in an unruffled tone of voice, "I am serious."

He looked across the table at her and wondered whether he should smile or not. The thought that she might be serious crossed his mind, but he refused to bring himself to accept that possibility. "That is not going to happen." He said, but in a tone which she recognized, which she interpreted to mean that he was confused; that he was prepared to give her words some serious consideration. He was surprised that he was coming round to thinking that she might just be serious and that this new development must be treated with no careless disregard. "No, it's not going to happen," he ventured to repeat, and added, pretending that nothing had stirred him, "Because you're not leaving to go anywhere."

"But, if I decided to leave you, Roy, you couldn't do anything about it. You couldn't stop me, Roy, I'm telling you." She chuckled as she watched his discomfort, the barely perceptible trembling of the hand that held the cup of coffee. "No, you couldn't do a thing about it."

The cup went slowly, ponderously to his lips and his brows came together slowly in a deep furrow as his customary tranquil features changed. "Couldn't I?" he said, but his mind turned over that morsel of information unable to make any sense of it. He wondered what had got into her of a sudden to-night. They had had their differences, yes, their sulking moments, but nothing as serious as this had ever been hinted at before.

"No, you couldn't do a thing about it." She repeated slowly, deliberately, trying at the same time to anticipate what would happen after this.

"Is that so?" He did not know what else to say, what else to do, and that annoyed him; rendered him impotent.

"Yes, that is so."

He smiled uncomfortably, wondering whether or not that query revealed his unsettled mind, his abject failure to comprehend what was taking place, what was happening to them.

She thought she would wait for her words to penetrate his consciousness before saying anything more.

Roy studied her for a moment, not yet wanting to take her at all seriously. She did not smile and her eyes when she looked at him betrayed a mind occupied with thoughts of a disturbing nature. This puzzled him the more. What was she up to? But, women are bitches, eh? She wouldn't of a sudden, so, decide on such a step, and mean it, surely?

Uncertainty, even a hint of nervousness, sounded now in his voice when he asked "What's the matter, Helen? Are you not happy here with me?"

The directness of her answer confused him even further. "No, I'm Not!" She returned the gaze which he had fixed upon her. She could be disconcertingly frank and blunt with her answers when she wished to be, that he knew very well. "No milk for me," she said when he picked up the jug. "Don't tell me you've forgotten already, Roy?" She laughed softly, mockingly as she looked at him. "I never have milk in my coffee."

His hand went involuntarily to his forehead as though to brush away some troubling thought, and he closed his eyes tightly not wishing to see whatever the vision that threatened to present itself. The thought came to him that this must surely be some game and that very soon he would see Helen smile and hear her laugh away his fears and his confusion.

"What's the matter, Roy?" she asked and teased him with a chuckle. "Got a headache?"

Take it easy, Roy, he told himself. Play it cool. Play it cool, now. "No" he said. "But you're talking such nonsense, such stupidity. I don't know whether to take you seriously or not." That's good, man. That's okay. Keep it cool. Don't let her rattle your nerves. Take it easy. This is alien territory, so keep cool and look out for the danger spots.

Helen smiled, but only with her lips, and even they appeared to sneer rather than smile. "Well." She said "you better think this one out seriously. Because I mean it. I'm leaving you, Roy."

"Look" he blurted out, unable to contain himself any longer, "this is all nonsense!" He had tried, but now his anger showed itself. "What the hell is the matter with you? What have I done to deserve this, eh? What have I not done that you've decided on this course of action?"

"Nothing, Roy. I'm just tired of married life, that's all. I want to fend for myself. I want to have a try, anyway. I think I know the way now. That's all. No other reason."

The furrows on his brow deepened, revealing the growing anxiety under which he laboured. No longer able to suppress what was uppermost on his mind, he said, nervously "But, I don't understand, Helen."

"No, I don't suppose you would understand. I've had enough of what I can take. You've done nothing wrong, Roy."

"Then…then, what is it? Is there someone else? I mean…Helen, you can be frank with me, you know."

Yet, even as he uttered those words it occurred to him how theatrical, how like a magazine piece of dialogue they sounded, and he hated himself for having revealed himself to be so immature.

Helen took another look at him and shook her head in pity for him. The age-old question, she thought, and in her voice she injected all the disdain that she could muster. "Isn't that just like a man!" She watched him recoil from the sharpness of her contempt and she pursued him further. "Can't think of any other reason but that there's someone else. Well, let me tell you, mister, there isn't! I just want to leave you, that's all." She became calm again, as though she needed no conscious effort to do so, for what she had to say next needed a clear mind. "I want you to understand that, Roy, I simply want to leave, to set off on my own."

"No! I won't let you spoil anything."

She laughed softly. "You cannot stop me, Roy," she thought to warn him quietly. He did not fail this time to recognize the note of absolute determination in her voice. "Don't even try."

He threw up his hands in despair, not knowing what now to say, how to accept this new situation which was unfolding before him. "There must be some other man. There has to be. Well, isn't there?" But the very question bothered him because he realized that he had revealed how pitiful was his dilemma.

More heartless in her resolve now, she retorted "That's all you men ever think of! You're all the bloody same! There has to be another man. Well, cock, there isn't! So there! You all think that all a women wants to do is to jump into bed with another man. Well, I don't! And you can get that idea out of your silly head. I just want to leave. To get the hell out of here!"

"Helen, sweetheart…."

"I'm telling you, damn it! You want to know, and I'm telling you."

The avalanche had come cascading down about him and in his heart he cried out to whatever personal deity happened to be responsible for him to disentangle him from this debacle, this enveloping tragedy. And like the helpless man in the face of danger, a danger he knows that he can no more forestall than the inevitability of death, who throws up his hands as though to stop the advancing catastrophe, Roy made one more bold but futile attempt. "I don't know why or how we started this argument in the first place. I don't want to hear any more about any of this."

Helen shrugged her shoulders. "That's up to you, Roy. But I've warned you. Don't say that I didn't warn you. I'm leaving, and that's final."

"Ah, shit!"

"Oh, dear. You surprise me, Roy. Such language. Watch it, Roy, or you'll get corrupted beyond redemption."

"Ah, you....!"

She laughed in mockery at him. "Oh, Roy, you should see your silly face."

"You think it's funny, don't you?"

Helen said softly "Not really. It's you who's not taking me seriously."

"Because you've been talking such rubbish, that's why."

"Alright, Roy, have it your way. But don't ever say that I did not tell you. At least I've tried to be decent about it."

She rose, smiling, and with a wave of the hand in a gesture of finality, she turned her back on him.

"Where are you going?"

"To bed....Goodnight, sweet prince"

He did not answer her, did not follow her. That night, for the first time since their marriage, he did not lay down beside her in bed. She heard him go out, observed merely that he had left the light on, then she fell into a deep sleep.

For more than an hour Roy walked the streets in the vicinity of his home, neither stopping nor slackening his pace. When he returned to the apartment the light in the sitting room was still on. The house seemed enveloped in a portentous silence. It had the effect of making him feel the loneliest person in the world. He undressed slowly, deep in thought, his mind awhirl with a thousand and one conflicting thoughts and emotions. For several hours after he had stretched himself out on the settee sleep eluded him. He heard the hours chiming away from a clock tower not far away, the last of which he was conscious was four o'clock

When Helen awoke in the morning she found him still fast asleep on the settee.

She did not wake him.

Chapter eight

All morning the events of the previous night occupied Roy's mind. His attention wandered unceasingly during the lectures and this annoyed him the more, for everything kept returning vividly, making concentration on his work more difficult. It rained persistently and methodically, as though the weather also was determined to drive home some vital point.

Why had Helen been so insistent that he tell her when he would be home? He had not known how to interpret her smile when she had seen him to the door. As though nothing had happened between them. Thinking about her and the night's events and trying to focus attention on what the lecturer was saying tired him, making his whole being so listless that he wished to return home. It would be better, he decided finally. To-morrow he would feel better after a good rest. He gathered up his notes and his briefcase and asked to be excused from the remainder of the lectures. He gave his reasons.

"Hope you feel better to-morrow."

"Yes, sir. Thank you."

The journey on the underground train seemed to him to have been longer than usual. The train stopped for a while in the tunnel and for a moment all was darkness in the carriage where he sat. When the lights came on again the carriage was silent save for the rustling of newspapers and the occasional cough from a passenger. The silence in the compartment, he thought, was as silent as a tomb. He imagine that's what it would like in the grave, silence save for the movement of the worms.

God, what a people! he thought as he looked about him at the faces, or more like masks, really, immobile and expressionless. No one spoke to another. Total strangers in the land of the dead. Tombstone city.

He was relieved of those morbid thoughts when the train arrived at his destination and he had the feeling of surfacing from the bowels of the earth, the abode of the dead.

The rain had ceased but the air was still damp and, except for the movement of vehicles there was no other sound, certainly not human. He encountered a few people after a while, but they were hurrying along about their affairs, strangers simply passing through this life unseeing, unseen and unknown to each other. Some lines from Byron's 'Childe Harold's Pilgrimage" came to him…. 'And thus they plod in sluggish misery, Rotting from sire to son and age to age, Proud of their trampled nature, and so die…'

A moment before entering the house he turned around to see if he would discover at least two people in conversation. No, not at all.

He thought the house was unusually quiet as he inserted the key in the lock, then he remembered. Of course, it was always quiet. He would take a hot bath, have a warm drink then go to sleep. Sleep and a little rest would do him good. Sleep for the mind and rest for the body. Strange, he thought, how, when the mind becomes restless, the body also became fatigued. He pushed the door open and something solid impeded it.

"Damn! What the hell is that?"

The three suitcases lay immediately inside the doorway. Inside Helen sat on a chair dressed as though ready for travel, her coats resting on another chair beside her. She rose startled and in confusion, but immediately Roy's eyes met her own she appeared to regain her composure.

Roy looked about him as if in a daze, unable to understand what was taking place. He pointed to the suit cases and looked at Helen. "What's all this about, Helen? Where are you going?"

"I told you I was leaving. Do I have to remind you?"

"Don't talk rubbish, woman!"

Helen smiled at him and at his having to raise his voice to her. "You can't frighten me, Roy," she said in a quiet, almost sedate voice. "I told you last nigh that I was leaving."

"And I'm telling you to stop talking nonsense, woman! Start unpacking your things! I've heard enough from you. Where the hell you think you're going?"

"I'm not unpacking anything, Roy, and you can't make me. I've already found a room, and paid the rent. I'm not going to remain here any longer. Now, is that clear? It's just unfortunate that you found me here. I was going to leave you a note thanking you for all that you've done for me. I shall be forever grateful to you. But I've had enough. Let me go out to prove myself. I want to go. I wish you would understand, Roy."

He did not hear her. The avalanche of anger and resentment had so overwhelmed him that he had become blind and deaf, had rendered him utterly and irresponsibly insensate. He took two steps towards her.

"I said unpack your things. Now! "

"No, I am not going to unpack. You can't make me stay here if I don't want to."

She wanted to brush past him and he took hold of her arm, but she jerked herself free of him. In an instant he acted so quickly and accurately that she reeled from the stinging blow, lost her balance and fell. She got up on her knees and groped towards the chair, stunned. She caressed the side of her face. They both realized in that instant that this was the first time that he had ever struck her. Their eyes held that expression of incredulity and final humiliation.

"You hit me, Roy. You hit me. Roy, you hit me!"

There was such sorrow, so much pained regret at the indignity to which he had subjected her, that he looked at his hand in disbelief, unable to bring himself to realize that he had done such a thing, that he had been reduced to such a despicable state as to strike a woman, something that he had sworn to himself that he would never do. Now it had come to that. The look in Helen's eyes told him that he had crossed the Rubicon. There was now no turning back for either of them. That realization of a sudden seemed to add flame to the anger in his heart, and Helen, sensing this, grew sorely afraid for the first time. She realized, also, that she had crossed over into territory where neither of them would ever meet again.

"I'm leaving you now, Roy, for good. I can never remain here after this. Never! You've disappointed me, Roy. I never would have imagined it. Now I know anything is possible."

"Don't provoke me further, woman."

"Oh, it's woman now, is it? I have always called you by your name." Yet even as she was saying this she felt in a way trapped. Whatever she had calculated, whatever she had judged his character to be, this was now a man entirely new to her. There remained only one way out of her predicament. She willed herself to added bravery and got up, determined upon a new strategy.

"Where do you think you're going?"

"To the bathroom. Excuse me."

He stepped aside to let her pass, then sat down at the table to rest his head in the palms of his hands. His head ached as though it was ready to split in several parts, and his body shook visibly. To think that he had been reduced to this!

He was unaware of how long he had remained seated at the table. Helen returned and he sat up, vaguely conscious that she had been away some considerable length of time. She said not a word to him as she picked up the first of her suitcases, then another and moved towards the door. Roy got up, slowly and hesitantly, and attempted to take the suitcases from her. She dropped them, screamed, and rushed to the window waving her hands frantically. Roy halted abruptly in astonishment and wondered whether she had gone insane. She screamed again and continued to wave her arms.

What? What was she doing? He had no intention of striking her again. Yet she had screamed. And to whom was she waving? Those questions occupied Roy's mind for the present as he stood looking at Helen.

A moment later he thought he heard footsteps, then a knocking at the door. He listened. Had he heard right? Yes, someone, indeed, was at the door. Then the door opened. Some seconds elapsed before he realized that it was not the landlord. "Yes?" He wanted to sound calm, to appear composed, and wondered about the intruder. Who was he? He asked "Who are you? What can I do for you?"

A second person walked in, a policeman in uniform and Roy realized that the first man was a plain clothes policeman. "What can I do…..? What do you want here?"

The plain clothes man walked into the middle of the room, his hands in his pockets. "This young lady sent for us. She asked us to come in."

"Helen? My wife….? She asked you to come in here?"

"Your …wife….?" The officer appeared puzzled, but only temporarily. He would not be made a fool of by this Black, but he had to be cautious nonetheless. "Your wife, eh? Well, yes, she sent for us. Some kind of trouble here, have we?"

Roy turned to look at Helen who was hurriedly collecting her belongings to take them out of the room. The two policemen looked about them, at the typewriter on the table, the bookshelves, the record-player shaped like a grand piano, the cocktail cabinet tucked away unobtrusively in a corner, the paintings and small African carvings on the wall. There was the faintest sneer on the police officer's face, the one with his hands in his pockets. The Blacks live well in this place, was the thought that came to him.

The two turned to Roy who, though embarrassed, was beginning to regain his composure. He could not make up his mind, for the time being, whether to hate Helen, or to resent her for what she had done, to what she had now subjected him. Where had he gone wrong? What had he done to deserve such treatment? From Helen, of all people!

"What's your name, youngman?" the plain clothes officer demanded, his hands still deep in his pockets. He did not try to conceal his aggression.

"Why didn't you ask my wife? She's the one who sent for you all."

"I think you'd better answer my question, if you know what's good for you."

The other laid a restraining hand upon his companion's shoulder. Alone with them Roy realized how vulnerable he would be were he to make any false step. He had no doubt that the one in plains clothes was only too anxious to have Roy say or do anything that would give him an excuse to put the Black in his place.

Roy took from his pocket a letter addressed to him from the University and handed it to his questioner. There were certainly other ways in which he could deal with those two men. For the present he would allow them to have their fun.

"And yours?" the constable asked Helen.

She told him. Presently the two officers were startled by laughter from Roy. The one who was writing stopped writing in his notebook and looked up at Roy. "Something wrong, son?"

Roy ignored the sarcasm in the man's voice. "Of course," Roy said. "You two are well aware that by coming here you're in the wrong?" He had not thought of that before, so taken aback had he been by all that was happening. Now it was his turn to have fun. "You all are acquainted with the law, no doubt? You realize that you have no right to enter my home like this, meddling in my matrimonial affairs?"

That was not how he would have said it otherwise. He hated now to pretend to be calm and polite in the face of such flagrant violation of the law, and he wished he had had witnesses.

The two exchanged glances. Clearly they had to deal with an unusual one here. They consulted in a whisper. Then the one in uniform took over. "Well, you see," he said, "your wife sent for us. We didn't know…I mean…one can never tell when one is summoned, what the problem is; how dangerous."

"That's alright," Roy said. "It's purely a domestic matter, so I must ask you all to leave."

Neither of the constables appreciated Roy's manner, that assumed superiority and, uncertain what to do about him, they pretended to having misunderstood Helen's approach to them in the first place.

"Oh, alright," the one in uniform said. "But, you must understand …we did not realize. We were only doing our duty." He hated having to apologize to the Black. "We're sorry for having disturbed you."

Roy smiled. The constables moved towards the door and Helen ran after them.

"Please, don't leave me here. I have to carry out my things first. Please help me."

The two hesitated, but long enough to allow Helen to gather up her things. They did not like to be told that they had defaulted in their duty and the one in plain clothes would dearly like to square up accounts with that Black. When eventually they left Roy closed the door silently and sat down again at the table.

Strange, he bore Helen no ill will now. Even stranger still, he discovered within himself, that he had no regrets at her parting. The pain he had imagined would have enveloped him did not come. He heard the door of a vehicle slam shut and he rose quickly to look out the window only to see the taxi move away. A moment later he retreated from the window and considered all that had taken place. With a shake of the head he knew that all was over. It was but an end to another chapter in his life.

Chapter nine

It was a cold, quiet evening and Roy was about to settle down with a book when the telephone rang. He recognized Delgado's voice immediately.

"Man, you've got a drink for me." That was how Delgado had informed him about the apartment that he had succeeded in finding for him. Roy laughed, pleased at last to be able to leave the hostel to which he had moved when the landlord, having heard of the visits by the police, and putting his own interpretation on the visit, requested that Roy vacate the apartment. Some overzealous and inquisitive neighbour had reported the matter, embellishing the report to make it more colourful. "You know something" Delgado was saying now "You're one lucky fellow, you know that?"

The apartment, occupied for the moment by a Jewish sculptress, would be vacant at the end of the week. She had found a maisonette in Stratford in East London, which would serve both as a studio and workshop as well as a comfortable home. Delgado had met her at a party and in the course of conversation he had learned of her intention to give up the apartment. He had asked her to speak to the landlord on Roy's behalf.

"That's how you get many things in this place," Delgado said.. "Contacts, man. Contacts. Agents never help you; they're only interested in taking your money."

Roy moved into his new apartment on the second floor of the house the following Friday afternoon. Two rooms, a kitchen sufficiently spacious to serve as a dining room as well, then a bathroom and toilet. The telephone rested on a ledge beside a large window which opened on to a street below. The bedroom contained two single beds which Roy thought was convenient whenever he had any guest. A landing from the corridor out from the kitchen led to the bathroom and toilet. Roy had to share the bathroom with two other tenants.

"That's what makes the rent so reasonable," Delgado told him. "That's why the Jewish woman left. She hated having to share bathroom and toilet. She was not orthodox Jew, though."

Some of Roy's belongings had remained unpacked and he took them out now for there was sufficient space for them. Within two days he had completed the arrangement of his rooms and he sat down now to survey his work. He smiled, satisfied with what he had accomplished. Now he would work at his studies with renewed vigour. There would be no one to disturb him.

Soon the days began to slip away, almost unnoticed. He seldom saw the other occupants of the three-storied building. There were occasions when he imagined that they were deliberately avoiding him, or the other tenants. When he confessed his observation to Delgado, his friend laughed.

"No, man. In this country that's how they people are. They keep themselves to themselves; they even build their houses that way. Have you not noticed? Self-contained. Cut off from their neighbours and the rest of the community. Not like us back home who live out in the open most of the time. Calling out to our neighbours as soon as we wake up in the morning." Delgado laughed again. "Until some disaster, or some threat to their sovereignty. They're lucky they don't have hurricanes, like us, every year."

Roy thought it strange that people were able to inhabit the same house, use the same corridor, even more intimate, the same bathroom, yet seldom encountered one another. Worse, tried desperately to avoid each other. He had often remarked their behaviour on the trains and buses, but in the same house! That seemed to him unnatural, uncanny, and he could not help feeling that people like that could never mean any good one to the other, or to the rest of the world.

He worked out a routine for he was one who believed in self-discipline. Each morning he rose at seven, made himself coffee, then to the bathroom to shave and to bathe himself. The bathroom served two floors, the one which he occupied and which he shared with an obese young white woman of about twenty-two or twenty-three, who lived in the adjoining apartment, and the floor immediately below him occupied by other young English women. Once Roy heard them bathing together and laughing and he wondered whether they were lesbians.

Afterwards he prepared his breakfast and read for a while, then set off for his lectures. Five days a week. Saturday and Sunday he woke up later. Yet always the house was enveloped in silence, as though it was desolate. Some days he fancied himself to be the sole inhabitants of this small world and he felt tempted to sing out loud to keep himself company. Once he did burst into song and even executed a few dance steps to a Mambo tune, but a Tock! Tock! Tock! From below with a stick caused him to stop to listen more closely. He laughed. It was as though a prisoner in solitary confinement wished to communicate with the outside world, a world he had joyously discovered was inhabited by another human being. The knocking came abruptly to a stop once he stopped dancing and singing, and he thought, so they are alive after all

Thus the days went by with Winter settling in with the mercilessly cold days and ever worse nights that Roy dreaded so much. The four o'clock darkness and the sun that never revealed itself reminded him also of the people who did the same. People coughing and sneezing and spitting their lives away as they traveled through the greyish whiteness of the fog that most mornings and evenings seem to envelop the world about them. People trapped in their own stultifying environment. The stench of staleness and the acrid smell of tobacco smoke from people who seem bent on a prolonged painful journey to their graves.

The frightening stories of the West Indian nurses and doctors who could not bring themselves to imagine how or why a people could be so coldly cruel to themselves. The countless deaths of the too-old and the too-weak; with people dashing off to work with only a cup of tea in their stomachs and collapsing like dead leaves falling off in the wintry gusts. "Go To Work On An Egg." the advertisements advised, but few seemed to take any heed.

He had witnessed one such death at the entrance to the Underground Station one morning. The old man simply collapsed and died, as though he had given up, had been fed up with life and wanted no more of this world.

Roy came to understand why the English people had wanted so desperately to leave this right little tight little island home; to travel enormous distances to new lands and to a more friendly climate. Why they had determined upon colonising other people's countries and to subject the resentful inhabitants to unspeakable suffering and unmentionable brutalities, rather than return to their island. In four instances they had chosen to exterminate the native inhabitants of those distant lands. They would attempt to make of those lands a little of Europe overseas.

Yes, he understood their dilemma and was even prepared, at times, to sympathize with them and did not begrudge their decision to leave.

He followed the doctor's advice and simple treatment and gargled the moment he got home, and washed his hands and his face with germicidal soap and warm water, and ate thick steaks and quantities of fruit juice. He never left the house of a morning without having eaten a substantial breakfast. All that cost him money, but he considered it money well spent for the retaining of his good health in this dreadful climate.

At last the Winter came to an end. March arrived with a burst of sunshine and the first buds of Spring. He welcomed the change, so did the natives who went about as though they had been shown the promised land, had been given a new lease on life.

He set about his studies seriously and Mr. Jameson, one of his lecturers who had shown an interest in him, was pleased with his work. One particular piece of work Mr. Jameson had set on Milton's 'Paradise Lost' which he felt obliged to read to the class. It was an essay based on William Blake's observation that 'Milton was of the Devil's party without knowing it.' Roy had set out to show that, unconsciously, perhaps, Milton had portrayed the Almighty as a dictator, an autocrat and that Lucifer, once the brightest star in the firmament, but later re-named Satan, had been portrayed as the world's first Democrat.

Lucifer had taken issue with the Almighty when he had called all his Angels together and had told them "Hear my decree which unrevoked shall stand. This day I appoint Messiah Head of the Angels." Lucifer's objection had led to the war in Heaven. Lucifer, now re-named Satan, had lost that war, but, according to him "He who overcomes by force hath overcome but half his foe," and that it was "Better to reign in Hell than serve in Heaven."

When they were last in Heaven, Satan told his followers, there had been rumours that the Almighty had intended to create a new creature called Man. He proposed that they return to Heaven to see if they would be able to upset the Almighty's handiwork. It would be a dangerous journey back, but, Satan told them, others among you might have different ideas. Speak. Let me hear you. Very different, Roy contended, from the Almighty's "Hear my decree which unrevoked shall stand."

Mr. Jameson put down the paper, adjusted his spectacles, then he smiled. "You may not agree with the interpretation which Mr. Francois has presented us here. In fact, some of you may feel violently outraged. Nevertheless, you must agree that it is rather refreshing to hear something new, some individual expression of opinion in defiance of all that has been said and laid down as final judgment on this matter." He looked about the room and asked "Has anyone anything constructive to say about this paper?"

They hesitated a while, one waiting for the other to begin. Those who had anything to say thought Roy presumptuous and came out in defence of religion. They did not agree with Roy that the portrayal of the Almighty was anything of a despot, or even an autocrat.

Roy listened to all that they had to say, smiling the while to himself. He thought that he had made it perfectly clear that Milton had injected into his poem the ideas fermenting in his time. They would have to re-examine the history of their country. Milton's time had been one of tyranny. It had been a time of differing political opinions. It had been a time of revolution and civil war. It had been a time, also, of the beginning of political parties and debates. How, then, Roy explained, could a writer who feels himself committed to a recording of the realities of the day refrain from portraying and commenting, in his work, upon the immediate problems confronting him and his time?

No, no serious writer would avoid the issues.

Roy, smiling, stretched out his legs in an attitude of relaxation. Their literature, yes, but he would interpret it the way he saw and felt it.

Chapter ten

The Spring rolled into the promised Summer and London smiled its welcome. Only young scholars wore the air of concern. For them Summer would come later. Ralph, a young man to whim Delgado had introduced him towards the end of the Winter, also had sat for his examinations. He did not wish to predict the results, but he had the feeling that he had not done too badly with the papers. He intended to leave England the moment he received his results. If he got through he would be away towards the end of August. He had his future all planned, he confided to Roy.

A study of biology, at twenty-four Ralph was tall and thickset with eyes that seemed always to be searching, penetrating into things. His hair, piled thickly on his head, gave him a wild and savage appearance, and he often remarked, humourously, that at home he never would have dared to go out like that.

That's what this country does to you, Roy thought. It breeds carelessness and indifference.

Ralph had the most sensitive hands that Roy had seen; it reminded him somewhat of Ruth, long and slender. They suggested to him the hands of an artist, and they were kept always meticulously clean. He appeared to move through the various strata of English society with an ease which several of his friends envied. He seemed to know everyone worth knowing and who would be of use to him later in his career. He, too, like Delgado, was fond of the films and had been given several small parts to play. When asked why he did not take to the medium seriously as a career, he would laugh uproariously as though that was the greatest joke ever.

"No, man, I'm not a homosexual. My business is still with women."

"I don't see what that's got to do with it."

"Ah, but it does." H said and laughed. "You live in a very protected world, I can see. You have no idea what goes on. Let me tell you some things that will shock you."

In his last small assignment he had played the role of an African chief. He had met a young actress on the set who had taken a fancy to him. She had talent, that he could see, and everyone agreed that she was good, but she would never make it to the top because she refused to pay the price demanded of her just to see her name in lights. She refused to be a mattress for the top boys.

Sometimes he would relate his exciting exploits at night clubs which he visited, or on the film and television sets, and Roy would shake his head in wonder and astonishment. He would wish, on occasions, that he were there, also, or that those things were happening to him. He would imagine situations and laugh softly to himself. Once he thought of Ruth and, remembering the softness of her hand when he had shaken hands with her that night at Delgado's, and her dark velvety complexion, and almost as though the scent of her perfume would come floating to him. He could see her smile, showing those beautiful white teeth and feel the warmth of her body enveloping him. Those thoughts would fill him with desire.

"Uhm!" he grunted, remembering, and Ralph laughed, imagining that Roy had heard what he had been saying.

"Yeah, man. This is one hell of a place. Really crazy, man."

"But, you're having fun, anyway," Roy offered, tentatively, hoping that Ralph would put him on the track of what he had been saying.

"Yeah, but it's not a place for us, for me, anyway, to settle. No, man. This place?" He shook his head, "No, sir!"

He did not intend to return home immediately he told Roy. He had conceived a number of theories which he wanted to investigate, and certain experiments that he wished to carry out in Africa. He had always argued, he confided in Roy, that Europe had never given Africa's medicine men their dues, the respect and recognition which they deserved. Scientists had left Europe to discover what was going on in Africa, expropriated the knowledge, then hurried back to Europe with their discoveries, and after a little experiment here and there, they would claim that they had discovered some 'new' drugs. Things that our forefathers had had in use for centuries were being publicized as European discoveries.

"Take the use of chlorophyll in toothpaste, for example, Ralph said. "We've been cleaning our teeth with guava leaves for centuries, then polishing them with powdered charcoal to give them that extra pearly shine. I suppose our ancestors chose the guava leaves because of its special sweetness. But they had discovered that chlorophyll was good for the teeth. Europe hasn't got round to utilizing the charcoal as yet. They'll 'discover' that later."

Roy had discovered very early in his acquaintance with Ralph that once he had launched upon any one of his favourite topics there was no stopping him. His ideas and his energy seemed boundless, so he settled down to what he knew would be a long session.

Circumcision, Ralph continued, was a peculiarity of the peoples of Africa, whether they were Jews or the tribes in Kenya or the Cameroons, it had been going on from time immemorial, long before Europe had come to 'discover' its value. Painless childbirth, certain fruits, roots, leaves and barks of certain plants which were being used to make people fertile or sterile, so long known in Africa, the Caribbean and South America, were only now being talked about in Europe. Such extensive knowledge of the medicinal properties of numerous herbs could only have come from a people who had achieved a high degree of civilization, and when one came to look closely, at sophistication also. The primitive only existed in the minds of the Europeans.

He had been investigating, secretly, the properties of the bark of a certain plant in the Caribbean which was used both in the aid of painless childbirth and as an aphrodisiac. Roy said that he knew the plant. One boiled the bark and diluted it to the required strength. He recalled the story of the man who had used it as an aphrodisiac but had not diluted it properly and had had an erection so rigid that the doctors had been unable to do anything about it. The man had died from a haemorrhage when the blood vessels had burst.

His investigation so far had revealed other interesting properties in the bark beside the known. He had to work in secret, he confided, because were for his European colleagues to discover what he was on to they might very well get ideas into their heads. And since they were Whites they would be able to raise the necessary money for their project. And. Well…..

Roy smiled.

"Man, you try going to the bank, or some funding agency with an idea like mine, as a Black, they'd laugh at you. But if you are White, then all doors are open to you."

Roy smiled. He had heard such stories before about the banks. "But, Africa." He asked, "will you be going back home?"

"Oh, yes, man. I'll never abandon those rocks out there. What? Miss all those fetes and those beautiful guitar-shaped women? You must be crazy! No, man, back home for me. I must lay down my bones in the Caribbean sun."

Chapter eleven

That Summer Roy travelled to the continent and visited Paris, Brussels, Rome, Geneva and Copenhagen.. He had thought of going to Eastern Europe, but when he mentioned it Ralph advised him not to do so. "Both British Intelligence and the C. I. A. would be after you."

"Not now, anyway" Ralph advised. "You'd be a marked man. Visits from the Security Police and all that. Too much bother. Ask the other guys who have done it, they'll tell you."

"But what for? Travel Agencies in London advertise holidays out there. America and Britain trade with them. They even build factories there and extend them credit facilities."

"I know, I know" Ralph said "I know all that. In fact those communist countries get more help from the West than our countries in the Third World will ever get. "Ralph paused and chuckled. "Come to think of it, you ever hear of any serious conflicts between the West and the Communists of Eastern Europe? No. The conflict, my friend, is between the West, the former colonial exploiters and our people, the Blacks. They'll accommodate the Communists, but not us."

"So, what's all the fuss about, then?"

"They're just not taking chances, that's all. Between the West and the Communists it's purely ideological. But between them and us it's a question of economic survival, and between former Masters and former slaves; between the exploiters and the exploited. Between injustice and fair play. They're scared stiff of us, because they think that when we get power, when we regain what was stolen from us, they'd be finished. That's it in a nutshell. And they cannot stomach the thought of not being the benefactors of black mankind."

"Ah, well," Roy conceded with a shrug of the shoulders. "If it's going to be all that trouble, I won't bother."

He wrote long accounts of his journey to Ralph. For the first time since he arrived in Europe he felt really and truly free. What a difference traveling to those countries made to him! It was like being on another planet altogether. Ralph smiled whenever he received the letters. The tour, he felt, would do Roy a world of good.

Roy returned during the last week of August and a jubilant Ralph, embracing him, imparted news of his examination success. He had already arranged to leave for Africa at the end of September. He had made plans for his farewell party. Roy made a brave show of being pleased, but already he felt a pang of impending loneliness at the thought of losing his friends and companions in London who had succeeded at their examinations and would be leaving for their homes in their various countries. He could not begrudge Ralph; he was on his way. And, after all, was not that the purpose for making the expensive journey to Europe? To equip themselves for the life ahead? He tried to imagine what life would be like without Ralph's and Delgado's cheerfulness, their sound advice, their endless tales of their adventures.

He had asked Mavis, a Trinidadian girl, to accompany him to Ralph's farewell party. She looked after an aged aunt who had brought her up. The aunt had taken a turn for the worse and Mavis did not think it wise to leave her on her own. She regretted having to miss the party.

"But I expect you'll be alright without me" Mavis said. "There'll be lots of other girls, I bet."

It occurred to him afterwards that he needed not to be lonely that evening. Ralph surely would have a number of his women friends there. Indeed, that evening he was never at a loss for dancing partners. Ralph introduced him to his latest girl-friend, an attractive black North American writer, Sarah-Marie who had had her first novel published and who had come to England on a Fellowship while she worked on her second book. She confided in Roy how very fond she was of the Caribbean, in particular the Caribbean rhythms which, she hastily informed him, were now the rage in New York – Calypso, Reggae, Soca. She liked Latin music as well. She wondered why she had not found the same enthusiasm in London. Except for Reggae, of course. Roy imagined that the 'rage' in New York probably had something to do with the increasing number of Caribbean people in that city, including Puerto Ricans and Cubans in Miami.

Roy was disappointed, though, that though Sarah-Marie liked the music, she could not dance. She had brought along a friend, Helen, whom she introduced to Roy.

"She's a much better dancer than I am," she told Roy. "And she's quite a character, too."

She laughed at the disapproving look that Helen darted at her. Roy was uncertain how to interpret Sarah-Marie's last remark. He decided that perhaps Sarah-Marie meant that Helen was an interesting person. A young man came to fetch her away, and while she danced Roy watched her every movement. Yes, she was an excellent dancer. He only half listened to what Sarah-Marie was saying to him. He thought he needed to be polite, but he could never bear to hear the North American accent. He could not explain why; he simply did not like it.

The music stopped and Helen returned to join them.

Sarah-Marie said "I was just telling Roy about that interesting conversation that we had last night, honey."

"Oh, that?" Helen said.

Sarah-Marie laughed. "Quite interesting. We must have another talk sometime, darling."

"If I'm in the mood for it," Helen said. She ignored the Italian who had come up to ask her for a dance. The man stood a little way off, waiting, like the patient persistent man of his race.

Roy found the situation intriguing. What would either of them do? The man waiting and Helen ignoring him. Looking closely at her now Roy thought her very attractive, with her oval face and her dark hair in fine curls adorned with those colourful beads. She was of a dark-brown complexion with eyes sparkling bright, except when she chose to be unfriendly, as she was doing now. There was something of the Indian in her. Since there were no people of Asian descent on her island, he assumed that she had Carib blood in her. That would make her taciturn, and violent sometimes. He liked her round slim figure. The backside and the bust were definitely African.

Sarah-Marie sought for something to say to fill in the gap that appeared likely to develop into an embarrassment. She had only known Helen for three months, but already she had come to discover how unpredictable a girl she often proved to be on occasions.

The man continued to stand and stare at Helen, waiting. Helen continued to ignore him.

"Roy is from the Indies, did I tell you, honey?"

What useless information Helen thought, but she said "Oh, I can see that." Trying to be polite.

It occurred to Sarah-Marie that Helen was in no mood for conversation just now. The presence of the Italian still standing there must have upset her. Helen appeared preoccupied, but still ignoring the Italian who now stood leaning against the wall on the other side of the room. A smile played on Helen's lips whenever she looked at Roy. Sarah-Marie thought she had better move away for a while to allow the two to get better acquainted.

"If you'll pardon me" Sarah-Marie said with a nod in the direction of the room where the drinks were being served. "I'll go get myself a drink"

"Right" Helen said and smiled as Sarah-Marie walked away.

The Italian remained where he was, and Roy, with a chuckle, observed "Looks like he's waiting for you."

"Oh, him. I promised to dance with him when I first arrived. He's been hanging around ever since. Let him wait. There are others he can dance with."

"Perhaps he prefers to dance with you," Roy said.

"Oh, yeah? He didn't ask my views about that, did he?"

"I don't know," Roy said, and laughed, a little nervously, thinking of Sarah-Marie's earlier remarks.

Ralph put on some new records and Roy invited Helen to dance.

"Perhaps he'll take the hint now" Helen said of the Italian.

"But, if you promised him…."

"I didn't say when."

"You women can be hard at times."

"You're right there." She laughed as she looked up at Roy. "You're lucky you're different, otherwise…"

"What?"

"Nothing" She smiled, and she was radiant once again.

Ralph had put on a vintage Perez Prado. To Roy it was like music from another age, another civilization altogether. What with so much Reggae and Soul and Funk, Roy was beginning to think that black people had lost their musical heritage.

The tune was 'Adios' and Roy tried to feel out Helen's movements, to gauge her reaction to the rhythm for he disliked bad dancers intensely, especially with Caribbean music.

He liked Helen's dancing, not absolutely perfect, but she had rhythm in her body.

"And what are you smiling at? " She was beginning to like him, so different she thought him to be. God! Didn't know they still had people like him around any more. So polite, so charming, it just wasn't true! Some woman will sure be lucky one day.

He let go of her, feeling safe with her and wanting to be on his own, to be free with his own movements. He was fond of improvisation, to give expression to whatever the rhythm stirred in him. He closed his eyes just for the briefest moment, as though something too delicious, too precious needed to be savoured in private for that instant.

Memories.

He opened his eyes, and as though delighted that the dream was true, that he had really found a dancing partner, he said to Helen "I like you."

She laughed.

She did not release his hand when the music stopped, and when another of Prado's masterful interpretation of the Mambo came on, he danced once more with Helen.

The number was 'Pachito E-Che.' Helen, too, had got into the mood of the dance. She closed her eyes, and her entire body, except her hands, which oftentimes stiffly, sometimes loose and simply dangling….all, except those hands, responded in some measure to the rhythm of the Congo drums. And in that Mambo, as in the Merengue, it is to the drums, especially the Congo drums, that one listens and takes one's rhythmical directions.

"Pachito E-Che! Baila el Mambo y el Son…"

The male vocalist sang on, his voice high pitched, passionate, invitingly sensuous.

"El gran sensacion" the vocalist called the rhythm and Roy would have defied anyone to take issue with the vocalist's choice of this descriptive adjectival phrase. The trumpet soared up and away until it seemed it would reach the stars. And the music lingered there a moment, quivered as though shaking itself free of some delicious reverie, and came wafting melodiously, sensuously down from that great distance, far away and sweet on silver-lined clouds, entering the body and coursing delightfully through very part of the body.

"Pachito E-Che! Es el grand sensacion…!"

Mambo….the eternal dance of life in the Caribbean. And like the Rhumba and the Beguine and the Merengue, saying something, expressing something, the age-old game of courtship and coyness.

Helen moved instinctively towards Roy and, as their bodies came together, they moved as though they were one.

Roy closed his eyes, savouring the moment. The music carried him away and across the Atlantic, and he was at home once again. It was a moonlit night. Beneath the spreading branches of the gigantic wild grape trees, he was with that sweet-voiced black girl with fire in her eyes and whose waist moved as though on ball-bearings, whom he had first loved. And as their naked bodies came together he could feel again the warmth of her engulfing him as he sought to fill her with what was overflowing from him.

"Pachito E-Che…!"

Helen felt the stiffness of him against her and she closed her eyes, resting her head on Roy's chest.

What Roy whispered to her was added music to her ears.

Chapter twelve

Of all the disturbing misfortunes, he had forgotten to ask for her telephone number. Sarah-Marie had left the following day for the West of England and there was no other way of communicating with Helen. He would have to await Sarah-Marie's return. Ralph gave him Sarah-Marie's London address and asked him to keep in touch with her for she seemed to be someone whose career was worth watching closely. Then Ralph left on the Thursday after the party. Roy accompanied him to the airport and stood for a long time on the observation platform, gazing despondently at the gradually receding aircraft. When it was no longer in sight he turned away and went home.

Slowly the days and the weeks drifted away and there began to settle in Roy's life a loneliness and a restlessness that he had never imagined possible.

One evening an old friend, Elton, an aspiring poet and playwright, telephoned to invite him to a party. He thought immediately of asking Helen to accompany him, and he wrote to Sarah-Marie hoping that she would have returned to London by then. She returned that very Saturday of the party and telephoned to Roy the instant she read the letter. She laughed when she learned of the purpose. She gave him Helen's telephone number and Roy telephoned soon afterwards only to discover that she had an engagement already for that evening. She was going to see a play by a young West Indian playwright and afterwards off to a reception for the playwright and the cast. She agreed, however, to meet him the following week-end at a coffee bar in South Kensington.

"You missed a great party" Roy told her when they met.

She frowned and sucked her teeth in disappointment. The party she had attended had not been at all a success, and she said, petulantly "Well, don't tell me when it's all over."

"I did try to get in touch with you, but I didn't know…."

"You did not try very hard, did you?" she said cutting him short so that he looked at her wondering whether she was really upset about missing the party.

"You didn't let me finish," he said with a smile. "I was going to say that I did not have your telephone number."

"But, Roy, you never asked for it."

"Well, I...."

She smiled at him. "Don't look for excuses young man."

"I'm not. I was going to say that I didn't know you...."

Again she interrupted him. "What did you say? You didn't want to know me?"

"Oh, don't twist things," he said, and feigned a laugh to conceal his exasperation. He imagined her to be playing a game with him, but only in jest.

"This is no laughing matter, my young man."

"I'm sorry."

"What for?" She, too, tried to conceal her laughter, but her eyes held a mischievous twinkle. "Well, never mind. Next time make sure you invite me well in advance, or else."

"Or else, what?"

"Or else we're finished."

"We've not started anything yet" he said, and laughed pleasantly.

"Well, we're not going to get very far if you continue like that." She paused a moment, then continued in a mood of reflection. "Still, I don't suppose you'd miss anything."

"You're a strange girl," he observed after a while with a short laugh and she asked him not to forget that.

Roy smiled, for it had come to him, of a sudden, that he was getting to like her very much indeed.

She looked about her and her gaze swept over the noisy youths, mostly French students from the Lycee opposite. She shook her head slowly at the snatches of conversation that drifted over to her.

"This is a very pleasant place," she said "but I don't think we ought to remain here to listen to that lot. So childish."

"Well, they're only children, after all," he said. He had been wanting to move away from there; it was only a meeting place, neutral ground. A question hovered in his mind, but he was uncertain how she would respond to it. "Don't fancy remaining here either."

"Well, then, shall we make a move?" she smiled and made as if to get up, but waited for Roy to answer. "Where to?"

He wondered about that question. "Well, we can go over to my place" he offered hurriedly, without a definite invitation, but it was out, anyway.

She looked at him a moment as though weighing the propriety of such a suggestion, and in that brief interval he thought of changing his mind. He hoped that he had not offended her. The way she was looking at him did not reveal anything.

"I was only thinking that...."

She interrupted him again. "Are you inviting me to your flat?" A smile played on her lips as she continued to look intently at him.

"I....I mean, if you would come, I'd be very happy." Because she said nothing he shrugged his shoulders to indicate that it really did not matter if she declined his invitation.

Then she laughed and he wondered about that.

"Well, it's a funny way of putting it, I must say." She paused once more and he imagined that she was giving the matter some further consideration. She glanced about her again as more students arrived with their noisy laughter and playful banter. "Alright. But you have to behave yourself, I'm warning you."

"What do you think I am?" He hoped that he sounded genuinely honest about his question.

"I don't think anything. I'm just warning you, that's all. I've met some boys like you....well, whom one dare not trust."

"Okay. Let's forget about it. I'm not sure that we understand each other." He rose to go, feigning annoyance and she looked up at him sharply. "It had seemed the polite thing to do. I was mistaken. Please forgive me."

"Are you withdrawing your invitation already? You have changed your mind, have you? Well, I like that!"

"You can call it that," he said and reminded himself not to smile.

"I told you I was coming, didn't I?" She smiled then, and stretched out her hand to him. "Come, let's be going, young man."

"Are you sure?" He was pleased, but went on to say "I'd hate to think that I was misunderstood, you know."

"Oh, I said I was coming. Come on, let's go."

He laughed softly and she smiled as he took her hand. "I like you," he said.

"I wonder how many girls you've said that to?"

"Oh, about a thousand and five, I think. I've lost count, really."

"Just as I thought." They were standing inside the doorway and as he paid the cashier, she said "Now, be a gentleman and help me on with my coat."

He laughed, and it came to him of a sudden that her bluntness must hide some weakness, or perhaps it was a defence mechanism. A strange girl, indeed. And all the way in the taxi and even when they arrived at the apartment the thought persisted, so much so that she became aware of his occasional lapses into silence which made her wonder what preoccupied him.

He assisted her with her coat and went into the bedroom to hang it up in the wardrobe. He saw her admiring the books on the three shelves and he stood just inside the doorway looking at her. Her back was to him and as his eyes traveled over her he wondered why he had not met a young woman like her before. Life would have been so much different. Lost in his own thoughts he was not even aware that, sensing his presence, she had turned to face him.

"Well," she said, turning to him with a smile, "don't just stand there. I see you have a nice collection of books, and a record player. Put on some records, then."

He said "Yes, I like both...reading and listening to good music." He laughed. "Well, music to my taste, that is."

"You have good taste, I must say. At least in books, anyway."

She confessed her unfamiliarity with the music of the Merengue, but she liked it nevertheless. He got up to dance on his own to show her the steps and she watched him closely, noting the insistent heavy downward beat of the drums which seemed to stir something down in the pit of the stomach, coaxing the hips and giving directions to the feet. The tune 'El Negrito del Batey ' (The little black boy of the sugar mill) came from the Dominican Republic, but Roy told her that he had bought the record in Paris.

"It's nice" Helen said. "Pity we can't get records like that here. All we get here is Reggae, Reggae."

Roy laughed. "They wouldn't understand that kind of music over here, anyway."

"I've noticed that unless they can play it and commercialize it they won't touch it."

"Even if we can play it and it's our music."

"Right. They're a backward lot, you know. Why should they give the black man a chance to make money out of his own music and culture?"

"You have a point there; they'll never give the Blacks a chance in this place."

"And if you tried to make it, they'll put a spoke in your wheel. Right?"

"Right."

Helen informed him that she came from a musical family. Her

grandfather had aspired to be a pianist, but there was no scope in a small island. Her father used to play the trumpet, until he lost two of his front teeth in a drunken brawl one night. That put an end to his musical ambitions." She looked at Roy and smiled. "So you see, I'm not exactly a stranger to music."

"I was only thinking that most people here are, even the young Blacks who were born here are different from us; they're almost British in their tastes."

"Not in music. You forget Reggae and Soul."

"Yes, but…."

"It's music, too, even though you and I may not like it too much."

He conceded that she had a point there and changed the subject. "Perhaps I was thinking of this indifference to Art. I mean Art with a capital A."

"If you mean that if you took them to task they wouldn't know what to say, what to look for, then I have to agree with you. But, only as far as the masses are concerned."

Roy looked rapidly across to her, then smiled. Perhaps Sarah-Marie had been right after all. Helen was an interesting person to talk to. It was rare to meet young people like her in this country he had discovered. He often wondered what they were taught at school. He smiled again, recalling what Delgado had said. "They teach them how to express themselves, but not how to communicate, so even their vocabulary is limited."

The records came to an end and Roy did not put on any more. He preferred to listen to Helen for it occurred to him that she might have something of value to impart to him. After all, he recalled, she had been living in this country from childhood, almost. She might have some clue to an understanding of what he might have overlooked. In life? Perhaps. He would stick to Art, which was of great interest to him after having heard Delgado and Ralph talk knowledgeably on the subject. He held that he interpreted Art the way it affected him. He was wary of people who tried to explain great art as though it had some permanent meaning for all time, and doubted whether Velasquez's denunciation of war would have any effect on present day Europeans to whom daily violence and brutality were now a commonplace. For that very reason he judged Art only in its relation to the present, informing a work of Art with a meaning that was only relevant to the way of life and thought of the contemporary generation. He maintained, therefore, that no one interpretation could be taken as being valid for a later generation. In that respect, all Art, to him, was modern.

Helen felt an instinctive affinity to this young man. For a time she had wanted to take up Art and to go to an art school, but her parents had dissuaded her. Of what use would that be to her, they had argued. So she had consoled herself with reading about many of the great artists and had perused some of the books on the esthetics of art and the philosophy of art history which she had found in one of the libraries in her Borough. She told Roy of some of the books that she had read—Mathew Arnold, Lessing, Arnold Hauser, Plato and some others. Her father never knew about that for she had kept those things a secret from him knowing that he would tell her it was a waste of time. But it had helped her with the crowd that she was going out with at the time, most of whom were either at the Chelsea School of Art, or the Central School, or somewhere.

She returned to what he had said before. "That may be" she said, and added that a great work of art, by which she understood Roy to mean a work that had intrinsic value, could only be understood by a very few people, hence went by default, for the masses whose reaction to the work and whose opinion would have borne any weight, remained ignorant of the moral struggles of their particular generation. "Such art" she concluded, "is priceless."

All this was music to Roy's ears. He was learning. He had found a real soul sister.

"Anyway," she said after a while "only a few people can understand and appreciate art."

"Why? Why do you think that?"

"Well, I think that great art is addressed only to those who had attained a certain cultural level. No, no! Listen." She hastened to add when she perceived that Roy was about to make some objection. "What I mean is, to understand great art one needs to have attained a certain level of sophistication; it has to be part and parcel of one's cultural environment."

"That is a wild statement to make" Roy said, wanting to tease her into saying more.

"Alright. Let's take this place, this country, for instance. Education, properly understood, is regarded as a privilege only of a particular class of people. The masses are too busy working themselves to death with overtime in order to make ends meet, and to pay their H.P. debts. How can these people find the time and the energy to...to ...cultivate any reasonable understanding of works of art? They can only go by what radio and television tell them, if they're fortunate enough to have the courage to listen to any such programmes, anyway. It's all weighted against them....time, energy, interest, education."

It was a tantalizing analysis, Roy said, but he warned her, nevertheless, against making such sweeping statements. "There's a danger in sweeping generalizations."

She laughed and challenged him to investigate. He declined the challenge. He had neither the time nor the inclination to find out what white people thought about the subject. He wondered, however, if it were not possible that they, what she called the masses, might not be willing to judge a work of art by other cultural criteria.

"You know what I mean? They might react to what is reassuring, or disturbing in it. Ever gave that a thought? To them that might be of value since it would have conveyed their wishes and their desires. They might feel a little more secure, or a bit more anxious about the course of their lives."

Helen doubted that Art could be a solution to anything and Roy was surprised by such cynicism, but he said nothing. He was more interested to hear her views which were all new to him, especially in a young person who had confessed to him of having so disturbing a childhood. People like that seldom had time for intellectual pursuits and he admired her for that. She had obviously put herself out in her reading. She said something about Art being to her only one aspect of reality and he wanted to hear more.

"Oh, yes?"

"I mean, what the writer, or the composer, or the painter had done in his work was not even to reveal any scientific truth, but merely to provide a guide which he thought, or hoped, could be used to combat the chaos that he beheld about him."

Roy shook his head and smiled, for she was destroying one of his cherished themes concerning the purpose of Art.

"You may smile, but I'm serious. I mean what I say. At least I recognize the false and the true."

The age-old question, he thought...What is truth? He admired her forthrightness and sought to discover how concerned she was about what they had been discussing, and said "You are fun...I mean, it's strange, really interesting to hear someone talk like that."

He laughed softly and said "Now I understand what I miss at my college. I often try to draw out the students in my class, but they react as though they were all dumb. I suspect that, really, deep down, they don't care about anything else but what they're studying." He paused awhile for reflection, then shook his head sadly. "You know, it is difficult to discover what really concerns them."

"I'll hazard a guess" Helen said. "They concern themselves only with what, for the moment, they happen to have been told, what certain branches of the media are pushing—South Africa and Apartheid, Race issues, Blacks and the Police. Books about them, documentaries about them. But those subjects are going out of fashion it seems, for I see now it's the turn of the Asians. It's always a fad; no intellectual depth or moral conviction."

"You've been here a very long time now, is it really always so?"

"That's how I see it. Most people here couldn't care for very long about anything, and that's the whole trouble with this country. So long as they can watch television, or listen to all that rubbish that radio sometimes put out, they can hardly be expected to care about anything, really. That crowd earlier on at the coffee bar, what had been their topic of conversation? You heard them too. The love affairs of mediocre film actors and actresses. Yesterday unknown, to-day it. Discussed, photographed innumerable times, interviewed incessantly by the media; their lives stories written up and absorbed by that crowd of empty headed nonentities, their meat and drink. Nonentities who set the fashion in morals and everything else. Drab life in a dull world made more so by a people bored to tears."

She laughed mockingly.

Roy wondered why no one had told them, for it occurred to him, listening to Helen, that those youths would continue to flourish in that tempestuous sea of make-believe and, sooner or later, end up battered and bruised for life. Helen's despair astonished him. "You'd be knocking your head against a brick wall. They've been so thoroughly indoctrinated that they've entirely lost the capacity to think for themselves. Slogans are what they understand. Anything to divert their attention from what really does matter. Look…"

From her plastic handbag she produced a leaflet that had been pushed through her parent's letterbox that morning. The leaflet, crudely printed, exhorted the white people in Britain to take up arms against the Black and Asian menace that was invading their country, depriving them of jobs, houses and their women: "COMBAT THE ALIEN MENACE!"

Not only the people of colour, but the Jews as well for, according to the leaflet, they were gradually and cleverly undermining Western Christian civilization with their cheap and shoddy culture which their Hollywood made films portrayed and with which they were drugging the white youths.

"Amen!" Roy exclaimed, and laughed. "Sounds almost like our present Prime Minister who said that the country was being swamped. Or something like that."

Helen looked sharply at him as though she were gazing at someone who had gone insane and ought really to be in an institution. "You're laughing at that?"

"What else can one do? I'm only here for a short while, anyway."

"You must be insane! Would you allow that to happen in your country?" She smiled when she beheld the change in his demeanor. "Ah! I thought not."

"In the Caribbean we do not talk in terms of race. We take the presence of other races for granted."

Helen was silent for a moment, as though considering what Roy had said. A moment later she said, quietly, almost as though to herself. "This sort of thing can be stopped overnight. Just as they stopped the Mau Mau, I heard my father say once to his friends. He said that the English people are very obedient. They've always taken their instructions from the top; never do anything unless they are told. But they…they up there, they won't stop it because they're on to a good thing. It serves good political purpose for the time being, my father said. It's a game that our people must learn to understand, I often heard my father say."

Roy listened, but said nothing. He was fascinated by what he was hearing. He said now "You must have learned a lot from your father."

He chuckled. "That's all the bastard ever taught me. Nothing else."

"Well, if anything, he has made a fighting woman out of you."

"You better believe it. Don't underestimate us black women, you know."

She had changed, he observed, for her whole expression was now one of intense alertness, belligerent, almost. "You see what happens when I really get going?"

"You father must be proud of you."

"Him! You must be joking! He doesn't care a damn about us, only about his politics."

He smiled at her. "Now I know what Sarah-Marie meant."

She waved a deprecating hand. "What's the time, Roy?"

"Oh, my goodness! It's almost one o'clock!"

"Bloody hell! And you let me go on talking like that? Why didn't you tell me it was getting late? No, how am I going to get home?"

"You mean you cannot get home?

"Don't be bloody stupid! Of course not! How the bloody hell am I going to get home at this late hour?"

"I had no idea….Time went by so quickly…I didn't realize…."

"Look I don't want any bloody excuses, Bloody hell!"

"Can't you get a night bus?"

"No night buses on Sunday mornings in these parts, you fool!"

"I didn't know, Helen."

"You don't seem to know anything about London, do you? Come on, think of something."

"Is it far to your home?"

"Right the other side. South London."

"Can't you take a mini cab?"

"I don't have any money. Do you?"

"Well, not enough" Roy said, after consulting his wallet.

"So what the bloody hell am I supposed to do?"

"Do you want to stay here until the morning? You can, if you like."

"If I like? I have no choice, have I? Did you plan this?"

"Of course not! Why should I want to do a thing like that? Do I look like the kind of person who would do that?"

"There's never anything special about them, mate. No distinguishing mark to warn us girls."

She saw that he was hurt, distressed, even.

He said "I'm sorry, Helen. I really am."

She laughed, then looked away. "Oh, alright. Never mind. It's not the first time, anyway. Better than having to walk the streets all night and being stopped by the police. and all these weird characters"

"What about your parents?"

"What about them?"

"I mean, won't they mind? Why not telephone them?"

"At this time of night? Are you out of your mind?

"But, what will they say when you turn up in the morning? Won't they be worried not seeing you?"

"Worried? They never worry about me, chum. I'm sure they couldn't care less. Wouldn't surprise me if they'd not be glad in a way. The selfish bastards! "

Roy was taken aback by such ill will towards her parents. "Helen!" he said. "Don't Say such things!"

"So? So I'm talking about my parents. One is my father and the other is my stepmother. So what? You want me to tell lies about them? That they care? No, thank you."

"Still, you must have respect for them."

"Of course I have! It is out of respect for them that I call them what they really are – selfish! Do you want me to call them what they are not?"

He stared at here in horror and surprise. That a girl should speak in such a manner was beyond his comprehension. He rose and took two paces away from her as though frightened to come into too close a contact with whatever had infected her. Why did she have to say such things? What was the matter with her? That sudden and violent change of mood and temper puzzled him even more.

"Well" she said after a while. "Am I staying here or not? Make up your mind."

Her demeanor when he looked at her showed that she was prepared for any eventuality.

"Yes, you might as well remain here."

"You're not doing me a favour, you know."

"Oh, for heaven's sake!"

He wished then to be out of sight of her for a while, at least until she had calmed down sufficiently. He feared otherwise that he might say something that might inflame her the more. No one, he told himself, ought to speak in such tones about one's parents. One's parents who brought one into the world? No. Who nursed one all through one's childhood? Never! What horrifying experience, the memory of which had compelled her to speak of her parents in such disrespectful a manner? He asked himself. He was unable to imagine what it could be. Whatever it had been he was certain that it was no justification for such unkindness. Not to one's parents. Never.

He said "I'll" prepare something to eat. You must be hungry." He felt that he had to get away from her for a while; to be with his own thoughts.

"Have you any cheese? I fancy a cheese sandwich."

He told her that he had sardines, corned beef, eggs, tuna fish…

She sighed, and gazed at him as though she were looking at a mentally retarded child. "All I ask was, have you any cheese?"

"No."

"Well, alright. Why did you have to list what you have. I didn't ask you that."

"So you would…..Oh, what's the use? Which do you prefer?" He felt exasperated now and wondered why he had become entangled with such a person.

She smiled. "A tuna fish sandwich will do, thank you."

"Thanks. I'll make it for you."

"That's kind of you. And a cup of coffee, too, please."

He nodded.

"Good. And don't be long about it, 'cause I'm hungry."

He went out of the room all the quicker to get away from her. In the kitchen he found himself smiling and wondering about the strangeness and unpredictability of women. Anyway, this one in particular. It occurred to him a moment later that all that show of bravado, all that outward display of brashness, was perhaps a front, a barrier that she wished to erect between a world that must appear puzzling to her. A kind of protection that she wanted to construct about herself against the vicissitudes of life.

Something else came to him, and when he returned with the sandwich and coffee he asked her "Tell me...you seem so well informed about politics and all that. How old are you?" She did not strike him as being more than twenty-two or twenty-three. He thought it difficult to tell for certain. She was beautiful, that he saw, and young.

She flashed her eyes at him. "Mind your own damned business!"

"Alright. Alright. "He smiled his apology. He could not tell whether she was at all serious. That he considered to be a grave fault with him, for a man ought always to know his way around a woman. "I only wanted to know. Out of curiosity, really. Nothing else. I'm sorry if I offended you by asking."

"That's alright, then." She smiled, and Roy laughed. "What's there to laugh about? What's so funny?"

"Nothing. I like you. I just like you, that's all. A little wild, perhaps, but I like you just the same. You're okay."

"Good, then. We'll get along fine. Right?"

"Right."

Chapter thirteen

She lay stretched on her back staring intently at the ceiling remembering how gentle he had been with her, how kind and how affectionate. No one, she recalled, had ever been as kind, gentle and affectionate towards her. And he was strong, too. Very strong.

She smiled and wanted more of him, but she did not want to disturb him as he lay asleep. So peacefully. She wished she could be as peaceful in her mind as he appeared to be. She would have liked to know what he was thinking about. The silence, however, began to play upon her mind. She wondered whether she ought to leave, but she did not want to, not yet, anyway, and that feeling pleased her.

So quiet in here.

Why doesn't he say something to her? Didn't he like her? Hadn't she pleased him?

Her gaze moved from the ceiling to the window through which the sunlight came streaming insipidly into the room. The curtains stirred gently as though someone had breathed on them. She began, almost unwillingly, to fear the silence.

"Roy?"

"Uhmm."

Oh, I thought you were asleep."

"No. Just thinking."

"What about?"

"You."

"Oh." She turned to face him and smiled at him. "You called me 'cherie.' Am I really your cherie?" She looked directly at him. His eyes were brown, she observed, and there was hair on his chest. "You called me 'cherie' and 'doudou' just now. What does 'doudou' mean?"

"Same thing," he said. He saw her smile and continued, "only a little more sweetness added to the 'doudou'"

"I like that." She laughed. "I really do." She wanted to get closer to him but he was so near but yet seemed so far away that she hesitated. "Do you always make love that way, so beautifully? I kept wanting you again and again. I never felt like that before."

He disliked intensely her reference to having known, or having had relationships of that nature with others. It was a habit with the girls and women in this country, he had been told before by some of his friends. It was so with the English women, but it seems that the black girls born in England and those who had grown up here had taken up the habit of discussing their love affairs and sexual relationships with their friends and even, on occasions, with their husbands.

Other thoughts raced across his mind, and he saw her now as the embodiment of her race in Britain, oppressed, underprivileged and who, unconsciously, were adopting European habits. Perhaps, his thoughts continued to run on, in their efforts to survive in their new home, their new social and cultural environment. Her parents generation had done their work, carried the burdens, rebuilt the country after the war, but had made no claims to a better way of life. They never thought of asking, of moving, even, in any new direction. That was because always they would be returning home next year, the year after. Then the years receded into the distance and they were still here, many having nothing to show for it.

In the meanwhile children, coming into a very different world, with different attitudes, manners and customs which the older generation of West Indians found it difficult to comprehend. Becoming alienated, lost, most of them, like driftwood in an open, unknown sea.

Roy watched her now and it came to him that there had been very little kindness and affection in her life. She had almost resigned herself to expecting nothing from life. Resignation seemed to have had a fate worse than death, for death, at lest, ended it all, whilst the other state reduced the being to a state of mental and physical paralysis.

A wave of tenderness swept over him and he stretched out his arms and drew her closer to him. She sighed when he kissed her. The sun, so rarely seen, hid itself behind a mass of dark clouds and when it reappeared sent its rays shooting once more into the room. Helen smiled and sighed again, happy because of her feeling that Roy's new understanding, expressed through his fresh embrace, had led to a discovery more momentous than the mere significance of the journey that she had taken so recently had envisaged. It occurred to Roy that what she needed above all else was love, affection, and help for whatever she wanted to achieve in life. He wished desperately to give that love, to assist her to be somebody in this adopted land of hers.

For her part Helen felt contented to be with him. She wished for no other. She recalled how she hated crowds, but how, equally, she disliked to be left alone. She would want him for her constant companion. If only she could visit him from time to time, that would be sufficient happiness for her, for in him she perceived a stability that she had never before experienced, nor had ever imagined she would enjoy. It came to her that if their relationship were to last long enough to enable her to acquire enough confidence in herself, then she would be well on the road which would give her life the meaning she saw that it could have for her now. For although she had come to recognize the causes of her dilemma of being black in a society of which she formed no part, which had, so far, conditioned her very existence, had so encompassed her, in fact, that until now she had had no view of a way of escape, or any means of hitting out. Except at her own, those close to her. The enemy was so elusive, the strategies so deceptive that one kept hitting out at the wrong target all the time.

She saw in Roy the person who would reveal to her the way out of her personal dilemma. She huddled closer to him and he enveloped her in his arms. For a long time they remained silent, enwrapped in their own thoughts, both wondering at the circumstances that had brought them together.

"Roy…..?"

"Yes?"

"What time is it?"

He turned and stretched out his hand to take up his watch from the small table beside the bed. "Ten o'clock."

She signed. "I suppose I'd better go home to have a change of clothing." He said nothing and she continued a moment later "I feel so comfortable here, so relaxed, so homely. I don't want to go, but I suppose I must." She looked over at him and saw the smile on his face. "Shall I return, Roy? I mean, do you want me to come back later?"

"If it won't cause you any upsets at home."

"I don't really care if it does. Really, I don't. But it won't, I know that."

Chapter fourteen

Helen returned that afternoon but said nothing of whatever had transpired at home and she appeared unperturbed about anything. Roy asked no questions, neither did he raise the subject when she began to visit him almost daily after that.

She was an attractive girl, but it struck Roy that sometimes she dressed inelegantly as though she did not care very much about such things. Perhaps no one had shown her or expressed any interest in her in such matters. A woman may never wish to admit it, Roy thought as he watched her, but it makes a difference when someone does care.

They became more and more attached to each other. Even so Roy found her still strangely unpredictable as ever. He sought to discover what her home and her parents were really like despite what she had expressed of her feelings towards them. She was particularly reticent about her step-mother. He had found out that her father's wife was not her real mother. Helen was not very fond of her either. She was grateful to her father for whatever little that he had done for her, but Roy had extracted from her that father had lost interest in his children a long time ago. Her step-mother had no children of her own.

"What did you learn from him, then?" Roy asked Helen one evening.

"Oh, mostly about politics, and music. You know, he even wanted to be a writer once."

"Really?"

"Yes, I only discovered that two years ago when I came upon some discarded manuscripts. I was really pleased. Thrilled, really"

"Why did he give up?"

"Rejection slips. But mostly because of my step-mother. She could never understand him wanting to be in solitude to do his work. She started going out and....well, you can guess what happens when once that starts."

"And he gave up altogether?"

Helen chuckled. "Nothing like disinterest in his women to destroy a man. After all, whatever he does, whatever he strives to achieve is for her approbation. Isn't that so?"

"What does your father do now, then?"

"I'd rather not talk about it." She was silent a long while, then she said "Sometimes we used to talk, or rather, he used to talk to me. Those moments were very rare, and only when his....wife was not there. I could not understand everything that he used to tell me .He used to speak a lot about art, though, I remember. He had some friends who were artists. One in particular he was fond of, I remember, a Jamaican. A short fellow with thick lips who was always smoking some small thin black cigars. He had large bulging eyes and he always wore a black beret."

"And he has stopped talking to you now, you say?"

Again she was silent a moment, then presently she said "I feel so lonely sometimes."

He looked intently at her. She smiled at him and confessed that he was the only young man to whom she could come whenever she felt so inclined, and with whom she could have a pleasant conversation.

"What about your friends?"

"Friends? I don't have friends."

"Sarah-Marie?"

"Only an acquaintance, really."

"You have no one?" He found it difficult to understand this.

"Have you seen the black guys we have in this place? Who would want to befriend and go out with that lot? One or two I thought I could have liked, but then, they turned out to be...Well, never mind."

He asked no more questions. He did not want to hear any more of her past experience. At week-ends he took her to the occasional parties at the homes of his friends. Never to the cinema. He did not care much for the cinema and would prefer to watch the occasional films on television instead. He took her to the theatre, if it was a play by a Caribbean or an African playwright.

"I get enough of the English stuff in the books that I have to read," he told her.

She was aware of the gradual change coming over her and she no longer felt any inclination to return home at week-ends. He asked if her parents ever questioned her about her absence, but she only repeated that they cared nothing about her, and since she appeared unperturbed, or even remotely distressed, he felt compelled to accept her words.

He could not help feeling, though, that a drastic change had come over his people over the years since their arrival in Britain. He had heard stories, but he had never paid too much attention to them. Now, confronted with this change of attitude towards family life, he was confused. This caused him to fear for all those who had settled in the country, even though temporarily. What would the people back home think who had looked to this country as the model to emulate? What a disappointment! Those who managed to return, especially with their children born in Britain, what effect would they have on the society back home? What new and alien cultural trait would they bring with them?

"Are you sure your parents don't mind you staying away from home?" Roy felt compelled to ask her once.

"I told you, they don't care."

"Do they know where you go, where you are?"

"Yes, I told them."

Her answer astonished him.

Their attachment to each other grew and strengthened after that. They became almost inseparable. Whatever attachment, however superficial, that he had developed with his other women friends he very soon loosened, and with those whom there might have arisen any jealousy he broke off contact altogether. A jealous woman could be absurdly and dangerously unpredictable in her reaction to the knowledge of a rival, of that he was aware.

He had been pondering those things one evening when the sound of the telephone across the room broke into his thoughts. He rose to answer and was pleased to hear Helen's voice.

"Hello, how are you?"

"Not good." He thought he recognized a tremor in her voice.

"Why? What's the matter? Anything wrong at home?"

"There will be."

"Where are you?"

"At home" She paused briefly before continuing in a lowered tone. "I can't talk here. I'm coming over to see you right away. Wait for me, will you?"

"Sure. I'm not going anywhere, But, what's the trouble? What's the mystery?"

"No mystery, Roy. Only what was inevitable. I'll tell you when I get there."

He replaced the receiver and puzzled over what it could be. Perhaps there had been a terrible row at home and her father had threatened to throw her out. But, surely, no parent would turn out a daughter whatever the circumstances. Yet, from what he had managed to gather from her so far, that would not be beyond the bounds of possibility. Well, he would have to await her arrival.

He went into the kitchen to put on the kettle for coffee, feeling a little put out at the disturbance to his evening's work. He had intended to write a paper on the Restoration Comedy of Wit in which he had been engaged during the past two hours. He was meticulous in his research for his writing that any disturbance was wont to make him irritable. The paper had to be completed before the week-end, and there was still that American textbook on the subject that he needed to read.

How the devils the Americans managed to produce such brilliant scholars, he wondered. No English writer, as far as he had discovered, except Professor Leavis, he conceded, had succeeded in anything comparable with what the United States brought out from time to time. To read an English text book, he maintained, was like grasping in the dark for a piece of black sewing cotton. He got the impression that the writer knew his subject well enough, but appeared deliberately to go out of his way to divulge nothing of immense value, to be deliberately obscure. He wondered why such books ever got published.

Take that man, for example - whose name he had forgotten for the moment – about whom so many had raved. A worse critic he had yet to discover. One had to read and re-read a paragraph several times before one could come anywhere close to an understanding of what the man was saying. Like reading Henry James, although he was American, but so thoroughly anglicized he could very well not have been an American. And he was not at all pleased with that anti-European attitude that he detected in Henry James. The critic, or the novelist, he held, ought to present his views clearly and unambiguously from the start. Communication was what writing was all about, not obscurity and headache.

He wished he had gone to the United States to study. It certainly would have been more fun. Or had remained in the Caribbean. But there was that widely held belief back in the islands that an education in Britain was the ne plus ultra of any achievement. How naïve! he thought. Any nation that publicized its institutions as being the best in the world must surely be suffering from some terrible inferiority complex.

He laughed softly at the idea that had occurred to him. Perhaps he was being too harsh with the British. They had produced Shakespeare, hadn't they? That alone was a superlative achievement. He laughed again.

Don't like the damned climate, anyway! He concluded for consolation and poured himself a cup of coffee.

Chapter fifteen

The doorbell rang once, but before he had time to get to the door the bell rang again, long and loud.

"Coming" Roy called out as he opened the door.

"What's the matter with you? Have you got cloth ears?"

Roy was taken aback by this unexpected assault and he stammered out his protest. "What...What? I...I...came as soon as you rang the doorbell. What's up with you?"

"We'll discuss that in your room, Roy. Let's get inside."

She pushed unceremoniously past him and he followed her, having first closed the door silently, pensively behind him. He looked intently at her as she threw off her coat, then sat down and proceeded to pull off her gloves slowly. He picked up the coat and took it to the wardrobe to hang it up and watched her again closely, still puzzled as he re-entered the room.

"What's the trouble, Helen? Who's upset you?"

"You won't be so damned patronizing when I tell you!"

"Alright, then. Tell me, for Christ's sake!" He was growing annoyed by her display of rudeness.

"I'm pregnant," she said and looked at him to watch how he would react to her disclosure.

"What....Wait a minute. What did you say?"

She chuckled as though in mockery. "What's the matter with you, man? Have you suddenly gone deaf or something to-day? Eh?" She flared up suddenly in a violent temper, but he could not refrain from disclosing his displeasure. "I said I'm pregnant! Pregnant! I'm going to have a baby! Damn you!"

"Alright. Alright." It was no use antagonizing her further when she started raising her voice. "Who for?"

"Jesus Christ! Who for? Who for, you ask?" She had shot out of the chair on which she had been sitting, her eyes wild, her whole demeanor so belligerent that he instinctively stepped back two paces from her. "God damn it! You stand there and dare to ask me who for? Who the hell you think been fucking me all those months, eh? Isn't that just like a man to ask such a stupid question! Well, man, I have news for you. Miracles of convenience like that don't happen in this modern world. That ended in Israel two thousand years ago. You hearing me?"

He recovered sufficiently to ask "Are you sure? I mean, it could be a false alarm, you know."

"Of course I'm bloody well sure! " She shouted her interruption. "You think I'm making this up? I've just come from my second visit to the doctor. Two months pregnant." She sat down dejectedly and began to cry, then gradually her crying became almost hysterical. "You brute! Why did you have to do that to me? Why? I didn't deserve this."

He had been standing a little way from her, and now he felt he had to go to her, to put his arms consolingly about her shoulders. "Please don't cry, Helen. Please don't make so much noise."

"Jesus Christ! Is that all you're worried about? Is that all?" She looked at him with such devastating pity that he instinctively stepped back from her. "Don't make so much noise?"

"Alright, alright. I'm sorry."

"Sorry? You'll be sorry alright, if you don't marry me."

"But...But, Helen...."

"There's no 'buts' about it, mate! You'll just have to marry me, that's all there is to it. Can't you understand?" She broke down and began to sob afresh, shaking her head miserably. "Oh, my God! What am I going do? What am I going to tell my father? He'll kill me when he hears about this. He'll kill me!"

"He'll understand when you explain."

"What?"

"I mean, when I explain."

"What the hell are you talking about? What will you explain, Roy? What will my father understand? You don't know my father. The only thing you'll have to do is to marry me. Do you understand now?"

"But...But...I can't! I mean..."

"You can't? You can't? Well you'll just bloody well have to! What the hell you mean you can't? "She raised her voice almost to a screaming pitch and he placed his hands upon her shoulder. She pulled herself violently away from him. "Don't touch me! Don't...touch me!"

He stepped away from her and at a loss what to do. "Don't cry, Helen, please. Oh, Christ! What a mess we're in!"

She continued to shake her head from side to side, repeating over and over "You'll just have to marry me, Roy. You'll just have to!"

"But I can't." The words having escaped, he sought to explain the impossibility of what she had asked of him, but he could only resort to a lie. "I can't because I'm already engaged to someone else back home. I can't break it off."

"Well, you'll simply have to break it off; that's all there is to it."

"But...But that girl...she has a child for me and we're going to get married as soon as I return home." One lie led to another and he was surprised how easily it was to do so. "I can't break it off, can't you see?"

"So! Is that all you do? Going about giving girls babies? Well, that's just too bad for her, isn't it? She'll just have to forget all about you, that's all. I don't give a damn about her! I am concerned about myself. Me. Period! And I say that you have to marry me. There are no two ways about it."

He was thrown into utter confusion, at a loss what to do. How can he get out of this mess? Suppose Helen was mistaken? The doctor? Well, what about the doctor? But how was he to know that the whole thing was not a ruse? But, why? Was it to get him for herself by any means? It could be.

"There's no such thing as got to" he said, calmly, while he continued to think of a way out.

"Yes, go on. Try getting on your high horse. You think that will get you anywhere? Well, mate, you better start making preparations, because when my father hears about this he'll hound you from here to eternity. And when he gets hold of you, God help you."

The tears continued to flow, washing away all pretence, exposing the awful mess that life had suddenly become. If only....If only....

In desperation he ventured a suggestion. "Look, I have n idea. We can get rid of the baby, you know. Then we won't have to....Well, look at it this way..."

"And ruin my health and my figure? No! " she screamed and shrank away at the horrible thought as though he had threatened to kill her. "No! No! No! Are you mad? You don't care if I die, do you?"

"No, you won't die, Helen. This is not the old days. Listen....No, listen...."

"No! I won't do it! I won't, you hear! How do you know that nothing will happen to me? Are you God?"

Her face, bathed in tears, revealed how dejected and miserable she was. He wrung his hands in despair. Certainly this was not a ruse. That he realized now. Sometimes a woman cries, and the tears are those of deceit, for a woman is strong, stronger than a man. She can bear pain, endure torment and even humiliation and, depending upon the kind of society in which she lives and of the place she occupies in that society, she can and may survive. But Helen's tears were those of hopelessness and overwhelming despondency. Haunted by the fear of what her father may do to her, may even do to Roy, she felt crushed and grieved at the awesome prospect of a man gone insanely jealous. She was too fond of Roy and wished that no harm come to him.

Roy, wondering what he would say to her father, knew how protective Caribbean fathers were towards their daughters He would be as nomadic in his sexual relationship with women, but towards his own daughter a Caribbean father would be uncompromisingly jealous and protective. Would their attitude change in this new social climate? It was that dichotomy in modern standards that baffled outsiders. In the midst of his dilemma now Roy had to admit that, were he a father, he would behave in the same way in protecting his daughter.

"Helen?" His voice came to her as from a great distance and she raised her head to gaze through the cataract of tears at the blurred vision of him standing before her. "Helen, do you want the child, or are you just afraid of what might happen to you if you were to attempt to get …to terminate the pregnancy?"

Even as he uttered those words he felt as though a javelin had gone through his heart, and his face became contorted with the pain. He had almost said get rid of it. Get rid of it! The very thought now horrified him. Who but a criminal would wish to terminate the life of a child? His first child. Her first child. And to think of such a thing! What kind of a society was this that forced one to consider such evil thoughts and even worse action? Was life no longer sacred? Did they no longer love children back home?

Ah! But how often had he heard it? This was not home. This society apparently does not hold human life at all sacred any more. Their wars showed that. It was a society in which morality and degradation had sunk to its lowest depths. Evil was accepted, and one evil led to another until only a system of moral and spiritual bankruptcy held sway.

He had heard enough stories to frighten him when he came to think about them. All those black girls cooped up with their babies in those Council houses, or in care. My God! Was this what he wished for Helen? It was all becoming clearer to him now, and he felt ashamed that he had spoken in those terms to Helen a moment before.

Helen had not answered his question immediately. When she spoke now it was as though from a great distance. "I….I…don't know. I want the child, in a way. And I don't mind being married to you. I mean…you've always treated me as a human being. It's the first time in my life anyone has done that. Sometimes, you know Roy, I have regretted telling you some of the things that have happened to me. But…men….the men I have known…have not been kind to me. You are so different, Roy, you have no idea. I shouldn't blame you alone for what has happened. It isn't fair. It's only….only…that I am afraid, Roy."

"Why? Afraid of what?"

"I can't tell….I don't really know…I don't know how I shall feel later towards you. I have to be honest with you because…because you've always been honest with me."

He left her side and began to pace the room engrossed with his own thoughts. She followed him with her eyes, observing how he clenched and unclenched his fists behind his back. She saw as well the deep furrows upon his brow and the darkness that cast a shadow over the lights that were his eyes.

She said "Oh, I know you will treat kindly, Roy. I'll probably never be happy with another man, if anything were…..But, oh! I don't know. Why has life to be so complicated, Roy? I want you…and yet…Oh, God! I'm so mixed up. Perhaps it's the way it's happening to me."

He stopped to look at her. He, too, was in a dilemma. All that talk about the profundities of life, art….what did all that lead to? What help was all that to them now? All talk, talk, talk. Theories. Now came the reality, and there was the dilemma.

He said, almost without thinking too much. "Then how can we get married if that's the way you feel? How can we?"

"But you must, Roy! You must! The vehemence of her language seemed to rent the air. "Jesus Christ! Can't you understand?"

"Alright. Alright. If that's what you want."

He would have done anything. Would have agreed to anything to have her cease those hysterical outburst, those heart-rending sobs. What a mess! What else was there to be done? He asked himself. His troubled mind sought for an answer, but neither answer nor consolation did he find. What kind of a woman was that who did not wish to do what she was forcing upon herself, and upon him, yet felt compelled to do so for no other reason than that society would punished her severely, one way or the other, were she to refuse to conform?

And himself? She was right. Of course she was right, he argued with himself. She is not the only one responsible for this mess. He could not truly hide behind any excuse.

"My father is a vindictive man" Helen was saying. "He….he would find a way to do something awful to you, I know. I am sure he would see to it that you lost your place at the university. He would concoct some story. He would take a delight in ruining you, your career. I know the man. He can be wicked! Wicked!"

Roy threw himself into a chair and held his head as though it was getting too heavy for him to carry upon his shoulders. Had Helen looked at him at that moment she would have observed how his shoulders shook, ever so slightly. He felt that he had exposed himself as a coward. When Helen needed him most he had thought of excuses; had resorted to lies, and now he felt ashamed of himself. How was he to face the future with the thought that would be constantly on his mind that he had let her down. How often had he confessed his love for her? And was this the way to show it in her hour of most need?

"It will have to be soon, I suppose," Helen said, intruding upon the turmoil that was overwhelming him now.

"What...? What did you say?"

"The wedding.....It will have to be soon."

"Yes, the wedding." He was wading through the muddle of bewilderment and perplexity. "Yes, I suppose so."

She wiped away her tears and the sobs were abating now. "Two weeks" she offered as a suggestion. "I think two weeks will be time enough to prepare. Not that there is anything to prepare for in this...this situation."

He shrugged his shoulders in resignation. "I suppose so."

"Don't suppose. Will it or won't it do? That's what I want to know.?"

Oh, God! What the hell has become of me? What have I let myself in for? What will I tell them back home? I didn't come here for this."

"Well?"

"Yes, it will do." He paused a moment and continued in a tone of utter dejection "I suppose you will have to get things sorted out with your parents. Will it be alright?"

"I will have to? What about you? You are in this as well, you know. Both of us will have to go and tell them. Right? So get that straight. You're not backing out of this."

"Alright. Alright"

"There's nothing else we can do", she said. "After all, they'll have no choice when they hear what we have come to tell them."

"When can I come to see them?"

Only when he had asked the question did it occur to him that she had never invited him to her home; had never before even suggested it, and that it had not bothered him. He recalled that at home he would never have thought of going out with a girl without getting to know her parents.

Here they had met, had got to know each other; her become intimate; had allowed their relationship to deepen and had given no thought to the likely consequences which might very well not have happened had he been on social terms with her parents. He blamed himself for having behaved so irresponsibly. He had to admit that.

Helen did not answer and he repeated the question.

"I don't know," she said. She would have to arrange a meeting. "I must time it properly, and break the news gently to them. It's my father I'm afraid of. When I think of how he used to beat my mother...Oh. God! I don't even want to think about it. What happened to her...to us...to our home...."

She burst afresh into tears, loudly now, and Roy looked on helplessly as though all strength had been drained out of him. He wanted to put his arms about her, but he remembered how she had screamed some moments earlier when he had wanted to do just that. He looked at her now instead and thought of how life sometimes played tricks on one.

Chapter sixteen

Roy did not look forward to his encounter with Mayfield, Helen's father. His apprehension had been based on what Helen had told him. Roy was surprised when the meeting took place for the man's behaviour appeared to him as somewhat uncharacteristic. Roy had conjured up a portrait of a crude, volatile, yet talented individual. Tall and thickset, his appearance struck Roy as forbidding, but it was long after the encounter that he came to the conclusion that the man was either shy, or uncertain of himself in the presence of his future son-in-law. Helen was pleased that Roy displayed such self-possession and that had seemed to have disconcerted her father somewhat. Roy saw neither Helen's step-mother, nor the other children, but he heard them in the adjoining room with the woman's voice raised every now and again in admonition of one of the recalcitrant youngsters

Mayfield apologized for not having anything stronger than tea in the house to offer Roy. He wanted to go out to buy a bottle of something, as he put it, but Roy dissuaded him; he would be happy with a cup of tea. Mayfield promptly left the room to ask his wife to prepare the tea. When the task had been done the wife called to him but did not herself come out, a circumstance that Roy thought was odd. He smiled at Helen when her father left the room and she returned the smile.

Helen had already made her confession and was baffled that her father had not been angry at all with her. Letting out a short laugh he had explained, as though in confidence, that there was not anything, really, that he was able to do in the light of what had been presented to him. He shrugged his shoulders, and said that he hoped that Roy knew how to take care of Helen.

"She's…..what shall I say? Sometimes a difficult one."

He laughed again, and continued, as though he was not really sure of what more to add. Well, she is often sharp with her tongue, hasty in her judgement, and….lazy. Perhaps Roy would succeed in getting her to make something of herself. She is not stupid. Oh. no. Even has some talent. Articulate, too, and loves the finer aspects of life, which he had been unable to give her. He wished, sometimes, that he had seen to it that she got into a university, or something. Maybe study literature or philosophy, or art. She seemed that way inclined.

Nervously twisting one finger round another he laughed once more, a short, halting laugh. He remarked, once again, that he hoped that Roy had enough money to look after a wife and child and still continue with his studies. He had always advised Helen to look out for someone with some substance.

His laughter, this time, revealed his embarrassment at such a revelation.

Roy sipped his tea to save himself the trouble of having to smile, or of having to say anything in answer to Mayfield's remarks. He studied the room instead. It was small and cluttered with furniture. There was also a small bookshelf, but he was unable to determine the titles of the books. He imagined them to be about politics, since that seemed to be his favourite subject, according to what Helen had told him. There were portable hand tools on the floor in one corner, but what struck Roy as remarkable were the two paintings on the wall opposite to where he sat. One was of black people caught in dancing movements. They were dancing to a man playing a Congo drum. The colours were varied and bright, the strokes bold but thin so that one had the impression of the dancers in silhouette. A carnival scene. The other was of a house beside a road in the countryside. There was a yellow poui tree in the background and a cow standing in a grassy patch eating nonchalantly while two black men in quarter length white trousers and bare torsos faced each other in a stick fight stance which reminded Roy of the Calenda. He turned briefly to look at Mayfield.

"Those paintings," he asked, "from home?"

"Yes. I bought them quite reasonable. I knew the artist. He used to live in London also, for a while. He came to see if he could make it here. As though a black man could ever make it in this country. However talented, they'll never let you. Never."

Roy was surprised at the passion in the man's voice. He wanted to say something, but did not know what. Mayfield did not venture anything further, and Roy turned to surveying the room again. It occurred to him, upon further observation, that the room was uncomfortably small, for he had received the impression now of congested space. The room now appeared to him untidy. A place like this, he thought, must present a problem to keep it clean.

When, later, he rose to depart, his gaze took in a vacant site that must have been the remains of a bombed out building. He wondered why it had never been developed. He could imagine Helen not liking such a place.

She walked with him to the Underground Station and on the way confessed how pleased she was with the way he had conducted himself.

"He's afraid of you," she said with a wry smile. "You must have frightened him. It must be. I've never seen my father so nervous, so much at a loss for words."

She laughed, amused that, at last, she had witnessed her father so restrained in the presence of someone who, without consciously demonstrating it in any way, had exuded good breeding and a superiority that commanded instant respect. She felt proud of Roy and she held on to his arm more firmly, more affectionately as they walked. At that moment she was sure that all would be well, and she looked forward to being with him for the rest of her life. Not without some tinge of regret did she recall the scenes in Roy's presence occasioned by her reaction that she was child by him.

"I'm sorry." She said of a sudden.

He turned to look at her? What for? What about?" he could think of nothing that she had done wrong this evening. Nothing that she had said.

"Oh, for the way I had carried on in your flat that day."

"Oh, that! Well....what else could you have done? It was only natural. You know, to tell you the truth, I didn't exactly help matters then, did I?"

"You could have deserted me. Go about your business. You know what I mean?"

"Well, yes. But that would have been dishonest. Worse, dishonourable. We...I mean, us black guys, we must learn to treat our black women with respect."

She smiled and snuggled up closer to him. "I'm glad I met you," she said.

Chapter seventeen

The wedding revealed a different Mayfield, one made expansive and gregarious with drink. He drank throughout the evening as though for a purpose. In his neat, well-trimmed light-brown suit he looked like a man who would have made good in any society that was equitable. But there was that about him which seemed to suggest that his excessive drinking was meant to conceal something—a failure, perhaps, that he did not feel man enough to overcome. It was a mood created by an atmosphere of hopelessness to which he had resigned himself. It was a feeling which Roy had often heard black people in London express with the words "Man, this country!" and which conveyed more than expletives would have done. He did not understand it. He did not know whether he wanted to understand it.

"I only came here to study, you know," was his way of dismissing the temptation to give too much thought to the problem.

Once or twice he had searched out Mayfield from amongst the guests to ascertain that all was well with him. In the short time that he had known the man he had began to like him. Perhaps one day before he left England he would get to know Mayfield better, for Roy was certain that there had to be something that was troubling Mayfield, something that remained to be revealed to a sympathetic soul.

He had changed his employment several times since his arrival in Britain, and was now a local government employee in a London Borough that had pretensions to be Socialist. Mayfield spent his money on drinks and tobacco, and his hobby, the building of toy ships. He had confessed that in his youth he had thought of taking to the sea and had had visions of himself as a great mariner, but his first experience of a hurricane at sea had dispelled all his illusions of the romanticism of the world of Joseph Conrad, his favourite writer, Roy was astonished to discover. He had wanted to do for his part of the world what Conrad and Maugham had cone for the East. On his bookshelf, on the few occasions when Roy had visited the house along with Helen, he had seen some volumes of the works of those writers as well as those of Evelyn Waugh, and a writer of whom Roy had never heard, Lafcadio Hearn.

There were also the works of Dr. Eric Williams, the Prime Minister of Trinidad and Tobago.

Roy's interest in Mayfield was aroused. He discovered that Mayfield hated anything and everything that smacked of the hypocrisy of the middle classes. For them in the Caribbean he had harboured the greatest contempt. A bunch of eunuchs, he called them. The words 'capitalist' and 'bourgeoisie' were constantly on his lips at the least excuse. He appeared to be in his element whenever the conversation turned to politics and he seemed to Roy to be sufficiently well read on the subject. Roy and his friends listened with absorbing interest, for many of the things he said made sense to them.

Later that evening Roy said to Helen "I see where you have received your education in politics. Your father is a most interesting man."

She chuckled. "I've been hearing nothing but politics from the time I learned to read and write. He's been at it, he told me, from the age of fourteen, so he should know what he's talking about."

"He should have remained in the West Indies," Roy said.

"He says so sometimes," she ventured, thoughtfully, "but I wonder at times, though."

Roy was silent for a while. "He could, though, here."

"I don't think so."

"Why?"

"Oh, it's a long story. He might tell you about it himself some day, if you're lucky. It is better he tells you himself."

Roy was intrigued. Mayfield appeared to have an answer for everything. No question seem to baffle him. He would quote from all the leading national newspapers, the week-end journals and the Sunday newspapers. He would mention books and writers about whom Roy and his friends, with the exception of Elton, had not heard. Mayfield would smile when his listeners confessed to their ignorance.

Elton asked him a question that had been puzzling him. "But, why aren't you in politics, man? You ought to have been doing something, contributing your share to helping black people in this country."

There was general laughter, for Elton had a way of making the most serious of subjects sound so humorous on occasions, that no one could help but laugh.

"Aaaah!" Mayfield said and wagged his finger at Elton. "I've blotted my copybook, you see." Then he laughed and repeated "Yes, I've blotted my copybook.'

"Oh, I see" everyone exclaimed, without the remotest idea what

Mayfield meant by that, yet each giving a multitude of interpretations to the remark with "Oh, I see."

Throughout the evening Helen's step-mother had remained aloof and uncommunicative while she watched her husband become more and more talkative and jocose. She was smartly attired in a turquoise coloured dress which clung to her shapely body without being remotely vulgar, and she was beautiful. Roy knew that she was young, but did not realize it until now how very young. Mayfield, he calculated, must be at least twenty years her senior. Occasionally she remonstrated with her children, more out of necessity to talk to someone, it occurred to Elton who had been observing her closely. Roy had caught him more than once looking in her direction.

"You've missed out there," Roy said to him, and laughed.

"What? Oh." Elton said. "She's beautiful, isn't she?"

"Now behave yourself, man," Roy warned, for he had seen the look in Elton's eyes and was not sure whether to be amused or apprehensive. "The woman is married, you know."

"So what?"

"Oh, Christ!"

Elton chuckled. "Okay, pal" he said and slapped Roy gently on the shoulder. "You know I'm a very discreet, man. Or, don't you know that?"

He went over to Mrs. Mayfield and Roy shook his head. "Jesus Christ!" he muttered to himself and turned to walk to the door where he saw that a group of people had come in.

They had not been invited and Roy did not even know them. He sighed helplessly. West Indians had an uncanny way of sensing a fete wherever it happened to be, and no matter how secret the arrangements were kept. Some of the young men had come in with bottles of drinks, another strategy that was almost certain to win them admittance and acceptance. Some had come with empty hands. They were gay and boisterous, adding fresh vigour to the party.

"Eh, eh, man! What's happening, non?"

"But whose fete this is? Who got married?"

At that stage, a complete stranger whose name Roy later was to discover was Delgado, made his appearance in an entirely novel approach which had everyone in fits of laughter.

Time Present

Chapter eighteen

He had taken Delgado's advice and had not sought her out. "No, let her go, man," Delgado had said. "Let her go. Once a woman takes such a step it's no use going after her. For a man it's easier. A man does that after a great deal of thought. You get her to return and you'll be at her mercy for the rest of your life, if she stays that long. No, my friend, if you ever want a woman for company you can always catch one in this place. They're like London Transport buses. You miss one, no fuss. Stay right where you are and another is bound to come along. That's my attitude, anyway.....Let her go, man."

It all seemed such a long time ago now.

Roy's faith in human relationship was shaken when he thought of how frail was the thread that held it together. A matter of months now, not yet a year and emotions, once so strong, were becoming only memories. Another page in the chapter of this thing called life which had only the meaning that one attached to it. Another will look at it and interpret it differently, failing to understand, even, what the fuss was all about. Such things were commonplace. Was that all there was to life?

He shook his head sadly. There was the life ahead that he had to face.

First he would need to get a divorce. How long that would take he had no idea. In the meantime he had also to complete his studies. In another year he would have been home. But now....? The questioned hovered, fraught with the menace of doubts and uncertainties.

He would have to tell them at home. What would his parents and friends say? What was he doing with his life? In three years he had run the full gamut of a lifetime? Was that what his parents had sent him to England to do? Would they not be disappointed with him?

He tried to put those questions from his mind.

He was on his way to meet Delgado and as he stepped out of the house he encountered the landlord. They exchanged greetings. Roy thought that it was kind of him to allow him to remain in the apartment until he had found another place. It would be difficult, the landlord had told him, to find accommodation in this city. Roy hoped that he would find somewhere with not too many restrictions, or where the rent would not be too high.

The landlord had come to him after the policemen had left and he had been upset by the whole episode. He had complained bitterly that such a thing had never before happened in his house, nor in the neighbourhood.

I have no way of verifying that, Roy had thought. I'm sure more things, and perhaps worse, have happened behind those closed curtains and locked doors. Still, he regretted having to leave the house with its silence and strange inhabitants who rushed back into their rooms like crabs, to hide, whenever they encountered one another.

Delgado had told him of a Polish friend, from the war days, who ran an Agency. Everything seemed to go back to the war days, Roy had come to discover, listening to Delgado. Perhaps, as Winston Churchill had said, that had been their "finest hour."

"They don't look as though they intend to have another war" Delgado had remarked cynically, once. "The way they were so quick to discard their friends, especially those who happen to be of a different complexion. You would never imagine that we had made any contributions to that war effort, the way they treating us black people nowadays. They better surrender next time, 'cause they won't have any friendly dominions left, black or white, to which to retire, as Churchill had been proud of saying to his people."

Roy had laughed then. "There must be one or two of their friends left," he said now "from the war days. The Poles, for instance."

"They were catching their arse, too, you know, even during the war. They made them do all the fighting. But the Poles saw the light early. They intended to make the British pay. How you think the Poles got all those big houses all over Kensington? Squatters. They had squatters' rights. They didn't buy them; not all of them. What they bought they got dirt cheap, because all them English people with money were taking off for Canada, Central Africa and the West Indies. Men I used to see, big white boys who ought to have been in uniform, they in short pants, pretending they were still studying. Anything to avoid going to the war. Man, that was one big scandal. Many, many fellers like me fell for that lark. We came to get killed while many of these English fellers were lazing in the sun." He paused to reflect for a moment, then chuckled. "Man, if we had had the foresight of the Poles, eh? And the Jews, too? Man, we'd be sitting pretty, pretty to-day."

"The Jews?" Roy asked. "What about them?"

"Yeah, man, the Jews, too. They didn't forget the British."

"How so?"

"I'll tell you. When the Germans were roasting and gassing them, these people here didn't give a damn. They were glad the Germans were doing the dirty work for them. They encouraged the Germans, if you ask me. And the Jews are taking their revenge now for their experiences in Palestine, too, after the war. Look about this place and see who's making all the money. Money like peas, man! They're not only making money, they intend to make one total wreck of English culture before long. And they know how, too. All I can say is, good luck to them."

Roy had read about Palestine. The problem was still there But, he confessed, he was at a loss to understand the rest of the argument.

"Aha! Well, anyway, I'm not talking politics to-day." Roy said. "The flat, man, or a room. That's what I am interested in."

"Okay," Delgado said. "Meet me here about ...eh...eleven to-morrow morning. I have a craft coming here to-night and I don't want to chase her away too early. You understand?"

"Right," Roy agreed, and chuckled. "I wish I were like you, man. You always taking things easy."

"Don't you believe that, you hear."

Roy shrugged his shoulders and Delgado went to the kitchen to fetch a bottle of whiskey and glasses. "Can't get any good rum in this place at all," he complained, pouring out a drink for himself and handing the bottle to Roy. "Is only that cheap poison from Jamaica they selling everywhere." He named the brand. "I used to know of a place in Harlsden where I used to get Mount Gay and Falernum, but they burnt down the place one night."

"Yeah?"

"Yeah, man. These people getting really bold, you know. But one of these days they will go too far."

"Right."

Over in the corner to the left where he had seen some books piled high on makeshift shelves stood a folding table and a typewriter. A sheet of paper stuck out from the machine and some loose sheets also were on the table.

"Like you started work again," Roy said, indicating the typewriter. He recalled that Delgado had told him that he wanted to write something about his experiences in England and during the war. In fact, he had confessed, he had already started to write it, but that nothing, after a while, was coming out of his head. "Yeah, man, I'm trying."

"The same thing?" Roy asked. "Or are you trying your hand at a novel, as you had told me once?"

"No, the same thing I'm working on. That's more serious." He did not know whether or not anything of the kind had been done before, by a West Indian, but he had started work on it. Then afterwards, he intended to write something about the black people's contribution to art and literature from as far back as he could possibly ascertain. "Homer, perhaps, down to the present."

"Very ambitious" Roy said. "That'll take a lot of research."

"Yeah. It's just an idea that occurred to me, that's all. I refuse to believe that any race of people has been put on this earth without having nothing to offer, without making some kind of contribution. What is ours? The world has been in existence for millions and millions of years! What has happened in all that time? Got my drift?"

"Right," Roy said, sipping his drink. The warmth in his stomach pleased him.

That was reason, Delgado informed him, that he had got interested in History and Philosophy. He had discovered Spengler. The book had had a tremendously powerful influence on black artists and intellectuals in the Caribbean soon after its publication after the First World War. He would discuss that some other time with Roy, he promised. When he had carried out his investigation many steps further.

He got up to fetch a slim volume from the pile of books and handed it to Roy. "Have you heard of him? No. Well, not surprising." After a chuckle he continued "Now, that is an interesting man from the Caribbean. Read it, You can read French, don't you?"

Yes. I read it better than I can speak it."

"That's alright, then. It won't be difficult for you to understand. Aimé Césaire. Talk about a man who is profound!"

It had come as a surprise to Delgado how far ahead of the British Blacks were the black intellectuals from the French territories. A glance at their works was sufficient to reveal how intentionally and humiliatingly retrograde was the English colonial system. One looked in vain for schools and could seldom find any really worthy of the designation. But forts and prisons there were galore! Oh, yes, the English were great administrators.

Delgado pointed to the volume in Roy's hands. "That man, Césaire, completely transformed my vision of the white world in which we live to-day."

There was also another writer, James Baldwin, an American Black, but his view of the white world was too bitter. I suppose that was because of his black American experience which happened to be violent in the extreme, too much fraught with physical fear to allow for any rational evaluation of man. On the other hand, perhaps Baldwin was an extreme example of the product of such a world, and it made him wonder what kind of a writer Baldwin would have turned out to be had he come from the Caribbean or West Africa.

Delgado saw that Roy had shown considerable interest in what he had said and he warmed up to his subject. Smiling the while, he went on to expound on his own theory of art and literature in society. Roy could not help observing, upon reflection, that Delgado's exposition bore more of a closer resemblance to his own than those expressed by his university lecturers who were not at all concerned so much with an interpretation or an elucidation of literature as with dates and anecdotes concerning the works and their authors. His essays on Milton, Swift and the Restoration dramatists were landmarks in a different school of thought that Jameson had been pleased to welcome in his own way as a challenge to the accepted methods of viewing and teaching literature. He had warned Roy, though, that he was not to divulge from the conventional when he came to answer the questions in the examination room. Whatever new or fresh ideas that he had on the subject he must set aside until he was on his way, so to speak. For it had occurred to Jameson that Roy's approach to the study of literature bore nothing of the established critics, as such, but more that of a writer examining the method, the technique which the particular writer under scrutiny had employed in order to produce the desired effect.

He said to Delgado "When I read Jane Austen and Thackeray, I saw how very much the English landed gentry depended for their wealth and style of living on the black slaves in the West Indies. But I have not met one English literary critic who has mentioned that."

Elton, he told Delgado, had told him once that it would have been more intellectually profitable for him if he had gone to Paris to read Literature. "That's their forte" Elton said. "That and Philosophy."

Roy had often wondered about that. Sometimes he thought that Elton was correct in his judgement. It had occurred to Jameson as well that Roy's ambition was to be a writer, and for that very reason he had not discouraged Roy's methods, but had merely cautioned him, with a little apologetic laugh, that the examiners would not at all favour Roy's individualistic approach to literature. Jameson was not himself one of the examiners, but he knew sufficiently well that if Roy wished to succeed then he would need to conform. That's how it was in this country, Jameson told him, he was afraid to confess.

Roy smiled, for here was Delgado confirming him in his view that he had first to achieve what he had come to England to do, and then he could settle down to the writing of his own ideas when he had set university life behind him. Delgado had opened new vistas to him, more than any university text book writer had so far succeeded in doing.

"There's a heap of work to be done in truth, you know," Roy said, speaking aloud what then had just then occurred to him while Delgado talked. "A lot of work, man, I tell you."

Delgado looked across at Roy and studied him a moment. "Yes. And I'll tell you something, you look after yourself, right? Get down to your work and forget that woman. Forget her, man. She has her own life, her own ambition that she wants to fulfill. You probably showed her the way, and she wants to try out on her own. Nothing wrong with that. Funny, eh? But there are people like that, you know."

Roy said "I'm not bothering about her, man. Not any more. She can kiss my arse for all I care. Who the hell does she thinks she is?"

"Right. That's the idea. That's the spirit. Have another drink, man." He poured himself a drink and passed over the bottle to Roy. "Women are bitches, I tell you. Bitches, man, when you meet the wrong ones. You know what? A woman told me once that a women can never starve in this country. She was right. Man, I could tell you some stories. Huh!"

"Cheers!"

"Cheers, man!"

Roy set the glass down on the table and rose abruptly. "Look, I've got to go now. See you in the morning. Right?

"Right, man. In the morning. 'Bout eleven."

When Roy left Delgado he resolved to work with greater determination at his task. Delgado, he felt in some positive way, had been an added inspiration to him. He brushed away all shadows of the past which had threatened to settle like a damper over him. Whatever the future held he would now regard as a challenge to be overcome. The first of these obstacles was the acquiring of somewhere to live. He felt he could hardly wait to settle down anew.

"To hell with you, woman!" he said aloud to himself when he reached his apartment and had had a bath and had changed into his pyjamas. "Who the hell you think you are? God's gift to the universe?"

He threw himself down on to the bed and went promptly to sleep.

Chapter nineteen

The room that Delgado's friend at the Agency had found for Roy was at the home of an elderly Scottish woman in Shepherds Bush, a Borough in the West of London where, he discovered soon afterwards, was situated one of London's most famous Teaching Hospitals. He did not care for very much for the locality, but he considered himself in luck, for the old woman, pleasant and helpful at all times, never allowed him to want for anything. She had a young daughter, blonde and rather attractive, who was almost of a recluse. From work to home and that was it. Her favourite past-time was watching television. Their religion was Church of Scotland about which Roy knew very little and cared even less. She had also a brother who was at Primary School. Only the old woman was the most friendly towards Roy. The other two, daughter and son were not unfriendly, they simply kept themselves to themselves.

Looking about the room he laughed softly to himself at the thought of Delgado and his helpful friends "from the war days, man." The man who owned the van and who had assisted with the removal of Roy's belongings happened to be an Englishman. Small and slim, he had been captured by the Germans during the war and, along with a small band of other prisoners of war, had made a spectacular escape back to England. How they had managed to perform such a daring feat, the man kept a secret. He wanted to write the story one day and did not want to divulge anything beforehand, lest some enterprising person got ideas about writing a film script or a television play about the escapade.

It struck Roy, looking at the man, that that war hero must consider that episode of his life his greatest moments. He was a bricklayer by profession, and Roy wondered what the man must feel sometimes going about such drab work after the excitement of the war and the dramatic escape. The man laughed when he related how he had been turned down for a job at the Post Office in Trafalgar Square.

"Bleeding marvelous, ain't it?" he said to Roy. "After what I did in the war and all that."

Roy suggested that his health, perhaps, must have accounted for that refusal. After all, what he had had to endure in the prisoner-of-war camp must have affected his health somewhat."

"Cor blimey, mate!" he cried out in disbelief. "What the bleeding hell you think it's like working out in the open all day? And I can withstand that and lots more, mate."

Roy shrugged his shoulders. "Such is life," he said.

The books presented a problem. He had never counted them, but looking at the six boxes in the corner he imagined there to be at least three or four hundred. He did not realize that he had gathered so many books. Delgado had introduced him to the world of black writers and to Russian writers as well and he had been scouring the bookshops acquiring what of their works that he could find. Now he had an impressive list and he felt proud of his collection.

He read avidly and gradually a multitude of ideas began to formulate in his own mind. Fascinated by one particular book by Aimé Césaire, he returned again and again to the slim volume, learning passages by heart. He felt proud that the Caribbean had produced such a man. Césaire was right; the idea of the barbarous negro was only a European invention. Why was the European always shouting about his superiority? Was he in such a frightful doubt about that and needed to convince himself? It must be so. And why were they to-day in England talking about a multi-racial society? Was it not because they were racists?

Roy laughed to himself, but too loudly, and stopped abruptly, lest the landlady imagined the worse.

He spent the days in quiet reflection of those ideas that his readings had engendered, and gradually the determination to succeed excluded all other thoughts from his mind, even that of the disintegration of his matrimonial life. He grew daily more anxious to embark upon his career as a writer and tutor. He would be able to combine the two. About that there was no doubt in his mind, he told Delgado one evening. He would regulate his life in such a manner that he would even have time to spare for socializing in the islands when he returned home. One of the first he would visit would be Martinique, then afterwards he would go to Haiti and Cuba. Whatever had happened in that island in its short turbulent history, Haiti, had always excited his imagination. What romance must reign there in those towns and villages! What a wealth of surviving African culture must there be to be discovered for his own benefit! And Cuba? Cuba was just another Caribbean island striving towards the working out of its own destiny. And that was of interest to him.

He threw himself into his studies with such vigour that before long

Helen became a name of the past. Whenever he studied his text books it was always with the thought now of making something more than of academic benefit of whatever ideas came into his head. Then he would spend an hour or two working on an article which he would send to a magazine in the Caribbean.

"They're not interest here in our affairs," he explained when Delgado asked him once why he did not submit those articles to magazines in England. "At least not those written from our points of view."

"Well, try the BBC, then. Why not? "

"No chance."

"I mean the Overseas Services" Delgado said. "Try them. You never know."

"I've tried them; the same story." Roy laughed. "No, friend. I have come to the conclusion that we will have to do our own thing. Start a magazine or something. Not me, because I won't be here that long to be able to help you all. You will have to do it on your own. I can send my stuff to the Caribbean. We have some good literary magazines there, you know. Barbados, Jamaica and Trinidad."

Once, he told Delgado, he had come upon an article on Caribbean culture by an English writer in an English magazine purporting to be written by a white authority on the subject. The young man had spent two years in Montserrat as an exchanged teacher of mathematics from the London Borough of Brent. He showed the article to Delgado and they both laughed over it. The man had understood nothing.

"Where is that place, anyway?" Roy asked.

"You mean, Montserrat?"

"No, man. That place, Brent?"

"Oh, that's in North West London. Willesden and Harlsden and Kensal Rise. That's where that chap is buried, Kelso Cockrane, the first West Indian black to have been murdered during the Notting Hill riots."

"Any black people live in Brent?" Roy wanted to know.

"Oh, plenty of them, man. Plenty."

"And that character writes such crap?"

"A lot of these white people are racists at heart, you know."

"Exotic dancers! Steel Band music a cacophony of noises…Calypso monotonous! The man is crazy! He doesn't know what he's talking about."

Delgado smiled and slapped him on the shoulder, "Don't worry about it, man."

It bothered Roy nonetheless and he launched into a discourse on

European dances that had Delgado fascinated. There was something lacking in them Roy maintained. The dances were devoid of meaning, unlike in African dances, for example. The movements in Europe were abstract and the dance had sacrificed its sacred and pantomimic character by being made to serve simply the erotic needs of the individuals. "Same thing in America. Have you noticed?"

The African and the Caribbean dance, Roy continued, warming to his subject, manifested the life force, and was never obscene. They had always meaning, for they held the world on its course. No gesture in the dances stood by itself; each was a symbol.

Delgado smiled and said "You should write a reply to that article, man."

"Ah!" Roy waved his hands in dismissal of the idea.

"I see what you mean," Delgado said.

Roy noticed an envelope on the table and went over to take it up. "I almost forgot to tell you about this," he said. "An invitation to a fete. You want to come?"

It was from one of those organizations devoted to the fostering of good relations between Britain and the Commonwealth peoples.

"Is it going to be a good fete, you think?" Delgado asked.

"Don't know."

Delgado did not appear at all enthusiastic. He sucked his teeth. "Those English people are such a drag at parties."

"I take it you don't want to go?"

"Man, I'm always in the mood for a fete. Why not? It could turn out to be another worthwhile experience."

"Good," Roy said. "I'll meet you for supper at my favourite spot in South Ken."

Delgado laughed. "I see you're learning fast" he said. Roy looked puzzled and Delgado explained. "Always eat before you go to an English fete. They never have food. Not soul food, anyway. Little sandwiches and cakes. Crazy, man!"

Roy chuckled. "You're right there."

The venue where they met for supper was one much frequented by students and the unemployed. Some of the unemployed spent their days between the betting shops, the public houses and the restaurant. The proprietor, a tall attractive brunette, did not seem to mind. She was married to a homosexual who had first worked for her as a chef. Her lover was a West Indian doctor who had a special way with women that fascinated Roy. They had become friends for the doctor, like Roy, was very fond of cricket.

There was a group of young Trinidadian young men in the restaurant when Delgado walked in. They were seated at a table close to the entrance. They surveyed Delgado's sartorial elegance and guessed that he was up to something exciting that night.

"Wha' happening, Saga Boy?" One of the Trinidadians asked.

And another enquired "Where's the fete tonight, man?"

A third laughed, for, always in search of a fete, that, invariably was Delgado. That was the first question he asked of any West Indian whom he encountered of an evening.

Delgado grinned. "Ah, boy! This is one fete you can't gate-crash."

"Like you circling high to-night, man?"

Delgado laughed. "But, how you mean! You notice, non? " He winked at his interlocutors and said "Partner, you'll have to come by Sputnik to join me there!"

Delgado looked about him. Roy had not yet arrived. He was about to select a table at the far corner when a solemn young man walked in. Black trousers, black polo neck shirt and grey jacket. He was from Belize,, a student at a drama school not far away.

"Hi, there, Hamlet!" Delgado addressed the newcomer. "How goes it to-night?"

"Cool, man. Cool."

Laughter. Then one of the Trinidadians intoned "What? Hast that thing appeared to-night?"

The newcomer's name was Clarence. It seemed that Hamlet was the only play by Shakespeare with which he was familiar, or that he liked most. Delgado had laughed when he had told him about Clarence.

"Wha' happen, then," Delgado asked Clarence, "you suffering from a complex, too?"

Clarence turned dreamy, puzzled eyes at Delgado. "What mean you, friend?"

Delgado suppressed a giggle. He said "It bothered Hamlet, man, to see his uncle screwing his mother. Any other man and it would not have upset him so much. But his uncle! And so soon after his father's death, too. He couldn't stand it."

Laughter filled the room. Someone observed that Delgado's was, indeed, a novel analysis of Hamlet's character, and wondered how he had arrived at it. Delgado did not reply for at that moment an Indian from Trinidad walked in with his English girl-friend.

"Eh, Brahmin!" Delgado called out to him "You not wearing your dhoti to-night? Wha' happen?"

"Look, man, ease me up, non," the Indian said.

"Brahmin don't wear dhoti," one of the Trinidadians volunteered the information. "Only Hindus."

"I know" Delgado said. "But, you tell that to him, non." The day before Delgado had been engaged in a discussion with the Indian on the failure of the West Indies Federation, and West Indian culture. The Indian had asserted that he was a Brahmin from India and had stoutly maintained that the Afro-Caribbeans had no culture, whereas the Indians had more than three thousand years of civilization behind them.

Delgado had tried to get him to understand that no people were without a culture of their own, but the Indian did not see the logic of the argument.

"So, you're a Brahmin, eh? Don't make me laugh, man. The Brahmins were never indentured slaves. That's how your ancestors came to the West Indies, as indentured slaves. You're insulting the Brahmins, man."

The Indian did not want to take on Delgado to-night; he had his new conquest to deal with. He settled her at a table and giving Delgado a pitiful smile, went to collect a plate of food and a glass. With the plate in one hand and the glass in the other he tried to open the tap to fill the glass. He wanted to show his woman how familiar he was with the place and did not have to ask for assistance. He succeeded in opening the tap, but in his endeavour to turn it off he was not so fortunate and the water spilled on to the floor.

Delgado chuckled. "What's the matter, Brahmin? Looks like you've forgotten how to operate a tap?" Encouraged by the laughter from the others, Delgado continued to tease him. "No doubt after three thousand years of civilization you've lost touch, eh? I suppose you all have special water pills now and taps have become obsolete?"

The Indian paused at Delgado's table in passing. He looked from Delgado to the girl. She smiled, not having understood the banter. It occurred to the Indian not to say anything that would antagonize Delgado.

"Alright, sweetman," he said. "But, ease me up. Non."

Delgado chuckled. "I'll tell you what. It will cost you a cigarette, though. Right, partner?"

"Right"

Delgado lit the cigarette. Roy came in then and Delgado waved to him.

"You eat yet?" Roy asked him.

"No. I was just having some fun there with my friend, Simon, the Brahmin while I was waiting for you."

Roy smiled. "You and Simon like each other too much." He studied the menu. "What would you like?"

"Whatever you're having."

"Right" Roy beckoned to the waitress and placed his orders.

There was time to spare and they ate in comfort, observing who came in and remarking what was strange, peculiar, or interesting about them. Delgado seemed to know something about most of the people who frequented the place.

It was getting towards nine o'clock when they prepared to leave. On the way out Delgado nodded to the Indian, Simon. "See you, Brahmin" he said with a wave of the hand.

Chapter twenty

"This is a good fete, man. What's it in aid of, anyway?"

"Some Commonwealth anniversary or other" Roy said. "I showed you the invitation the other day. Remember?"

"Yeah. Yeah. Oh. Yeah. I forgot."

Roy could see that the answer mattered little to Delgado whose eyes were roaming about the large room. He muttered something to himself which Roy did not hear.

"What?"

"The right people, too, it looks like."

Roy glanced sideways at him, and chuckled. He had heard Delgado hold forth on the iniquities of the class system in England, but he suspected that, secretly, Delgado cherished a soft spot for the people of "good breeding" as he would sometimes say, and a "good address."

"I thought you had reservations about them," Roy said.

"Yes, but let's face it, man. You can't beat them. I mean, without them this country would have gone to the dogs long time ago. What are the working classes good for but for canon fodder? I've no time for them. They're the ones who are against us. You try to put them right, and they don't want to know. So, why worry about them. They're not going anywhere."

"See you" Roy said. "I see a girl over there that I would like to dance with."

Right"

His eyes followed Roy for a moment amongst the dancing couples, then came to rest on a young Indian woman sitting at a table with a friend. With a start he noted how very much she reminded him of another young woman of many years ago. It fascinated him. How could two women of different races resemble each other so much in structure and features, one Indian, the other a Black. Or was it because he wanted to see a resemblance? To remember? Memory is a haunted tomb, he had read somewhere in a poem.

She was only nineteen, he recalled, and he had recently turned twenty-one. Her father was a barrister and the mother a school teacher.

He had volunteered to serve in the Royal Air Force and was on his way for training in Canada and was spending his last few days in the island before his departure.

Some nights, high up in the clouds, he had often thought of her. Berthilde was her name. She had always a smile for him, but they had never met, socially. Then one night they had met, very much by accident at a dance.

He shook the thoughts abruptly from his mind. The band, a group from Mauritius, had stopped. They played beautifully, both Western music and their own rhythm, one of which, very closely resembled the Calypso. He wanted to find out what it was. The Soca, he was told.

A moment later the band struck up again and the Indian girl who had caught his eye rose to sing at the microphone.

The saxophone remained silent for a while, only the trumpets, muted and trance-like, haunted the room. A flute followed when the trumpets ceased, and then back came the muted trumpets. Now the maracas and the bongos joined in, with the bass trailing nostalgically in the background to play its important but unobtrusive role.

Couples took to the floor.

The singer appeared to caress the microphone, her voice siren-like, her eyes half closed. Delgado had never heard the song before, and he stood entranced,

"C'etait hier...."

Her voice seemed to caress the words, evoking a mood. Presently those who were happy thought back to the day, the place, the very circumstances which had given birth to that happiness. Those who were sad recalled fond memories of pleasures long gone now, and sighed for those moments from the distant past. They recalled those moments, and the day, the place, the very occasions became so vividly, so rapturously alive that it appeared, indeed, as though, as the song said, it was only.....yesterday......

"C'etait hier, il y a longtemps,
Et tu te perds, dans la nuit de temps.
Que m'importe de saviour ou tu est,
Puisque tu ne reviendras plus jamais,
Simplement pour que mon coeur aie moin froids,
Simplement je te revoies... "

Delgado fancied that the singer's eyes, when she opened them, were upon him. He tried to put that other image from his mind, but it persisted, and he saw, in the girl at the microphone, that other form from long ago, and he felt once more the softness of breasts, the lips raised to his, the excited beating of the heart. Black hair, and the scent of delicate perfume…..He recalled that one night from long ago, as though it were, indeed, but yesterday.

He smiled at the singer, and she returned his smile.

The thought flashed through his mind again and he thought…Memory is, indeed, a haunted tomb.

Roy had disappeared from the hall. He returned and sat by himself at a table, sipping from his half-filled glass of whiskey. He, also, Delgado saw, was wrapped in thought as he listened to the Mauritian girl. With a voice like that, Roy thought, she ought to go places. He recalled Delgado's warnings about such things. They seldom made it in this place. Certainly not the big time and the big money.

"Those whites," Delgado had said, "they learn a few chords on the guitar and they say they're musicians. The drummers keep bashing away in a monotonous one-two, one-two-three beat, and they call that, too, music. Crazy, man!"

The band struck up a slow tune and Delgado walked over to the table where Roy sat. "What's happening?" he said. "That's a nice woman, eh? What a craft!"

Roy nodded agreement. "That's the only place outside the Caribbean," he told Delgado "where they speak the French Creole. Mauritius. I read that somewhere. Did you know that?"

"No."

"The only thing is that they're almost all Indians there."

"That's cool," Delgado said. "I'm partial towards Indian women. I got used to them in the Caribbean."

"Oh, yeah. But they're different back home. They've become creolized. They're like us. No sweat. We're Caribbean people, all of us."

"I take your point. This is the genuine thing, right?"

"Well, not quite. They, too, have been tampered with. The genuine ones are out in India."

"That's too far to go."

Roy laughed.

Delgado said "Right. It's good to hear you laughing again. Listen, are you game for a fete to-night?"

Roy looked up at him, but made no answer. He waited for more information.

"Some tests I met out there want to continue this fete at their home afterwards. What you say about that?"

Roy shook his head. No, he did not feel so inclined.

Delgado was never one to say 'No,' to an invitation to a party and looked questioningly at Roy. "You sure?"

"Yes, I'm sure."

Delgado shrugged his shoulders. A man, he thought, had to undergo a multitude of experiences during his short span in this world. Sometimes he weathered the storm without it leaving any permanent scars. He did not want any scars on his friend. It would be a pity, his thoughts continued, to have this young man of such fine qualities, who had revealed such promise, destroyed and his talents lost forever. He had seen many young men in his time go to wreck in this city. And young women, too. Often mere girls. He would not like anything to happen to Roy.

"If you change your mind, let me know. Okay? I'm going. Boy, there are some good looking girls in here, eh? Let me see what I can catch. See you."

Roy said nothing. Only gave Delgado a nod as he left. He emptied the glass of whiskey in one gulp, then went out to the toilet. He looked at himself in the mirror, straightened his tie and returned to the ballroom.

A Steel Band had taken over, a small six piece professional unit of men in middle age. They started to play a Bolero Roy watched Delgado lead the Mauratian singer across the floor. Roy had not heard a Bolero in a long time, certainly not since he had arrived in England. The tune reminded him of a beautiful young black woman in Costa Rica who one night sang the most beautiful Bolero that he had ever heard, 'Ninguna Manera.' It seemed such a long time ago and such a far away country. He recalled that for long afterwards he would tune to Costa Rica to listen to the radio musical programmes. One night he did hear her again. She was introduced as La Perla Negra, the Black Pearl. For a long time the sound of that beautiful voice would haunt him.

Costa Rica, Caracas, Cuba, Puerto Rico and Martinique, he recalled, put out the best musical programmes. The names of the bands brought back a touch of romance – Louis Alfonso Lorens, Perez Prado, Les Anges Noirs. The Black Pearl....they had been pearls, indeed, real gems, those beautiful songs that came from her lips.

England! What an ossified place this country turned out to be! There were moments when he wondered why he had come to this part of the world. "What the shit are we doing here?" he would exclaim in those moments. It had certainly destroyed all his illusions. England, a country that he had learned to love when he was growing up in the Caribbean. Europe had been stripped of all its pretensions; the Blacks had exposed them for what they really were, and they could not take it. To be so uncovered by their former slaves and serfs was too much for them.

Ah well! He shrugged his shoulders. Yet, secretly, Roy admired them. Their persistence in spreading certain aspects of their culture in the lands and amongst the people whom they had conquered. School children singing 'Land Of Hope And Glory.'

He remembered an Indian film that he had seen, but could not recall the title, where, in the midst of overwhelmingly depressing poverty, a village band had played 'It's A Long Way To Tipperary.' Crazy!

The music stopped and Roy watched Delgado return with his dancing partner to her table. When she had taken her seat Delgado bowed, oh, so gracefully to her, that Roy wanted to laugh. Another young woman also came to sit at the table. Roy looked at her with interest---dark hair, low cut black dress. Delgado came over to join him. "Nice girl you were dancing with," Roy said. "Nice, too, the one with her."

Delgado laughed. "Her name's Veronica."

Roy looked at her again. She could not have been more than twenty or twenty-two. Of medium height, round and slim there was a delicacy and a freshness about her, an aura of enchantment that reminded him of a newly opened Hibiscus flower at sunset. Her complexion, too, was like that of the Hibiscus. There was something else about her that told of gracious living, those refined features. He imagined her skin to be soft as well and he wanted desperately to make her acquaintance and wondered how to go about it.

"She's nice, man," he repeated to Delgado. "Really nice."

"You like her, eh?"

"You can say that again."

"Well, we'll see what we can do. Maybe we can persuade them to come to the fete, eh? At least I'll try," And having said that Delgado went over to where the young woman was sitting.

"Crazy!" Roy thought as he watched Delgado walk towards the table.

The Royal personage, the evening's guest of honour, had left and now all inhibitions were thrown aside. The Steel Band struck up another tune and laughter reverberated round the spacious room.

Roy heard her laugh when Delgado spoke to her. There was something distinct about that, also. Light and gay, and as inviting as the sound of tinkling champagne glasses on a moonlit night in the tropics. Why moonlit, he did not exactly know, except that she appeared so beautiful in the glare of the brilliant lights that now flooded the room.

Tropical moonlit nights, with the embracing sea breeze. He decided to store those impressions of her in his memory.

The band was playing a tune that had been requested by someone. A young man went over to invite Veronica's companion to dance. Roy wanted to go over to Veronica. He wanted to, desperately, but he hesitated. A man was going over to her, but Delgado reached her before him. She rose to dance with him.

He was all charm and elegance as he danced. Not once did he cease talking, never for a moment did he stop smiling. It seemed to Roy that there was another side to Delgado that he had not discovered before now. He wondered what his friend had found to talk about that seemed to interest the young woman so intensely, for she was looking at him and never took her eyes off his smiling face, as though she wanted to hang on to every word, his every gesture.

"You certainly held her interest," Roy said when Delgado joined him later.

Delgado laughed.

"What were you all talking about?"

"Aha!" He laughed again. "I'll tell you another time. But...she can't come to the party."

"Oh."

"How about you? Do you want to come" Have you changed your mind?"

"No."

"Okay. Suit yourself."

Roy felt disappointed somehow; jealous, even. He wished he had not hesitated in asking Veronica to dance with him. Frustrated, he walked away without telling Delgado that he was leaving.

In the taxi taking him home he felt he had acted somewhat silly and wished that he had not left so unceremoniously. What would Delgado think of his behaviour? Perhaps he ought to explain to Delgado when next they met. Of a sudden he felt he needed to explain, to open his heart to his friend. He would go to-morrow to visit him. For the moment he wished to be alone with his thoughts...about Veronica.

Delgado was not at home when Roy called. And for three days after that there was still no word of his whereabouts.

Veronica! He must be with Veronica. That's it, was the thought that occurred to him. He berated himself for not having thought of that before now. That's why he was so secretive at the dance. He would tell him another time, Delgado had said. Well, he did not want to hear all the sordid details. How could he do this to him when he knew how he, Roy, felt about Veronica? How could he do this?

On the fourth day when he called the housekeeper told him that Delgado was at home. She let Roy in, but was concerned that the young man, normally so polite whenever he came to visit, had brushed past her so discourteously.

"Thank you, I'm sure!" she muttered to herself and disappeared into her room in the basement.

Roy bounded up the flight of steps to the first floor. Delgado seldom locked his room whenever he was at home. If the door were shut now he would know that something was amiss.

The door was unlocked and Roy walked in, expecting to see, he did not know what. Delgado sat at his desk writing. Beside him was a glass from which he had been drinking. He signaled to Roy to take a seat while he finished whatever he was writing. Roy sat down in silence. Conflicting thoughts troubled him. What if he had misjudged his friend?

Delgado stopped some minutes later, read over what he had written, then turned to face Roy. "What's happening, man?" he said.

"You tell me, mate. You're the one who's been hiding."

Delgado laughed and rose from his chair to sit himself in another closer to Roy. "It's like that sometimes," he said. "I get an idea and I lock myself in and work at it. I tell no one. Not you, nor the house-keeper. I'm incommunicado. I shut out the world and envelop myself in my world. I like it that way."

"And that's what you've been doing?" Roy queried.

"Yeah. The book's coming along fine. Just fine." He got up to fetch a bottle of Mount Gay rum and Falernum and a glass. "I discovered a place in Paddington where you can buy the Falernum." He fetched a bowl of ice from the kitchen. "Help yourself, man."

Roy had been studying him in silence, those confusing thoughts still with him. He felt annoyed to find himself in such a state. He had not touched the bottle.

"Help yourself, man," Delgado repeated, looking over at Roy and wondering about his pensiveness. "What's the matter, man? You don't look quite your usual self to-day. What's up? What's happened? Anything troubling you?"

"How is she?"

"Who?"

"Veronica?"

"I have not seen since that night."

"You sure you haven't seen her?"

"Hey, man? What's wrong? You fancy her, don't you? Well, that's great, man! Time you got yourself straightened out."

"Answer me, man."

"Hey…!"

"Well?"

"Well what? Jesus Christ, man! What's the matter with you? "

"You were with her, weren't you?"

Delgado did not know whether to take Roy seriously or not. It was not like his friend to behave in such a manner. He wondered whether the events of the past months were beginning to affect him. That, and the added pressure of his studies. It was bound to affect the strongest person at some point, that kind of combination.

"Well, weren't you?" Roy insisted. "You're always after the women. I saw how you were looking at her."

Delgado shook his head sorrowfully. "You've got it all wrong, man."

There was in his voice, Roy thought he detected, something that suggested sadness and hurt. A lump rose in his throat when he took stock of what was being enacted before his very eyes. His heart gave a sudden leap forward, and a coldness such as that which fear and profound apprehension bring, traveled lingeringly and painfully through his body. He reminded himself that he must not, on any account, say or suggest anything that would upset his friend further. He had heard of cases like this, where the person only needed just that fraction of a nudge to push him over the brink and towards insanity.

He recognized that Roy hovered between that delicate balance, and told himself that he needed to be careful. His hand trembled imperceptibly as he took another sip of his drink. He had seen many young Blacks end up on the scrapheap of mental institutions, but it had been as though those occurrences had been remote tragedies about which he felt distantly uneasy. Roy's case was different. This young man was close to him. Roy was his friend, yes, and he was concerned.

Delgado put his glass on the table and pushed some loose sheets to one side before turning to Roy again. "No, man" he said "you misunderstand me."

"I came to you to get the truth, not stories."

"But that's the truth, brother man." Delgado was beginning to grow reluctantly impatient. "I have no reason to tell you otherwise." He was aware of the increasing impatience and he thought that it sprung from finding himself having to defend allegations made against him. Christ!

"I thought you would say that," Roy said.

Delgado did not wish to upset Roy, but he felt that his impatience, his exasperation was justified now. "Look, my man. I don't know what's the matter. What your problem is. I'll even try to help you if I only knew what's wrong."

"There's nothing wrong with me."

"Well, then. Cut out this cross-examination nonsense! I'm not in the mood." Delgado's displeasure appeared to startle Roy. "I've had enough of that, man. What the hell!"

He rose, picked up his glass again, and began to pace about the floor, transferring the glass from one hand to the next.

The outburst brought Roy back with a start. He lowered his head, afraid that he was making a fool of himself. He did not want to do anything of the kind, and certainly nothing that would make him lose this one friend. His mind was a fog of doubt and suspicion which he hated. .He shook his head and passed his left hand hard and slowly across his forehead and his eyes as though to clear his mind. He paused a moment with his head resting in the open palms of his hand, and of a sudden a loneliness such as he had never known before threatened to overwhelm him.

"I'm sorry," he found himself saying to Delgado and without raising his head, the words barely above a whisper. "I didn't mean to upset you, man."

Delgado, uncertain whether to say anything meaningful, looked first into his glass, and then at Roy. In the silence that ensued Roy heard him sigh, a long inhalation, then the slow, protracted expelling of breath that seemed to suggest a problem resolved. Or was it pity, perhaps, Delgado thought, uncertain, even, of himself and his own feeling.

Roy waited for Delgado to speak, but Delgado said nothing, only continued to look at Roy as though working out what to say or what to do.

"I'm sorry, man," Roy said, and there was such a look of despair in his eyes that the other turned away in embarrassment.

"It's alright, old chap," Delgado said." That's okay."

"I don't know what got over me. I really am sorry."

"We all go through rough patches sometimes. That's life."

Yet even as he spoke those words Delgado felt as though he was not saying the right thing. It was certainly not his way. He hated seeing anyone close to him in despair, for it was despair that he perceived in his friend's accusation. Wanting desperately to hold on to something that would give him a reason to hope, he had imagined that the more worldly man had taken that away from him.

"Let me pour you out a drink, man," Delgado said, and went back to his desk. He put in some ice cubes in a glass, poured in some Falernum and then the rum. "Here, taste this. Is it okay for you?"

"Yeah. Thanks."

Delgado nodded his head in relief, glad that a crisis had been averted. He did not want anything to sour his creative spirit at present. Not when everything was moving along so nicely.

"You like that Veronica, eh?" he asked after a while, and smiled at Roy. "She's nice, man. A real beauty."

"Like crazy, man," Roy said. "Like crazy!" He remembered her smile when she had looked at him at the dance.

"She told me she sings at a club off Baker Street. What's it called again? She told me. Let me see." He paused a moment, trying to remember. "Oh, yes, I remember now. The Blue Lagoon. Do you know the place?" Delgado laughed. "What am I saying? You don't have time to lime in such places."

"No, but I'll find it."

"Good. Do that."

"I'm sorry I was so…." Roy began, then stopped.

"That's okay, man."

"Thanks."

"For what?"

"For the address of the club."

Delgado looked at him, quizzically this time, and said "It's about time you got yourself a woman. A good woman."

When Roy left an hour later, Delgado stood in the centre of the room, looked about him and smiled.

"It will do him good," he said to himself. "Ah, Roy! Life can be a bitch sometimes, but don't let it get you down." He poured himself another drink, went over to his radiogram and put on a Calypso by The Mighty Sparrow. He sat again in his chair, threw his head back, and with his eyes closed, let the song and the music transport him to the Caribbean.